The FALLING Duet

Shirl Rickman

The Falling Duet

Falling Slowly
Free Falling

Copyright © 2016 by Shirl Rickman

The Falling Duet \ Shirl Rickman – 1st ed.
Library of Congress Cataloging-in-Publication Data
ISBN: 9780999368510

FALLING *Slowly*

For Mama and Daddy,
who taught me
love can overcome anything
and coffee makes the
world go 'round.

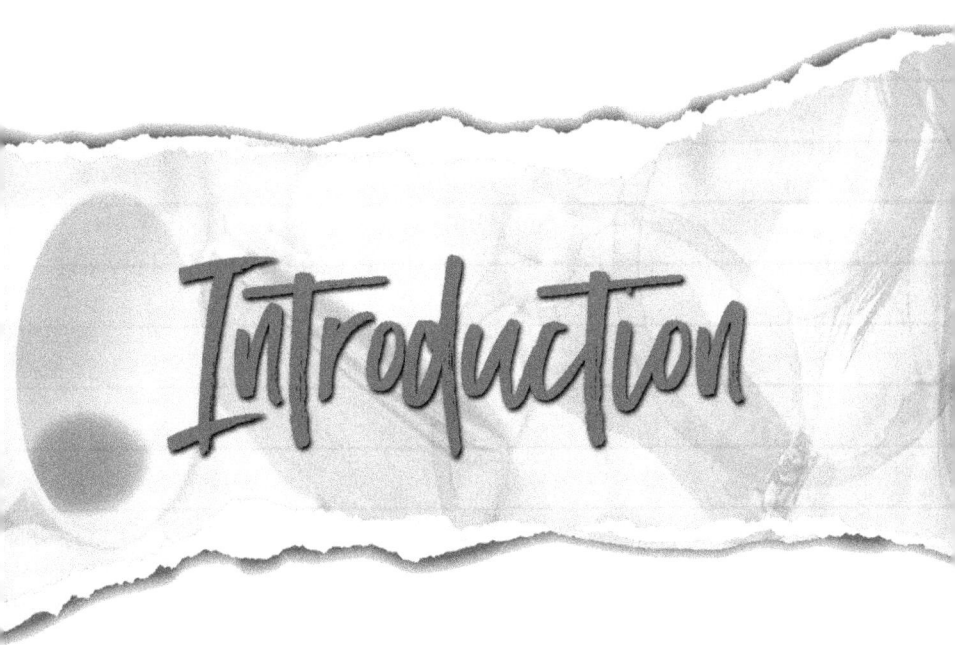

Introduction

My name is Rose. Rose Marie Fisher, to be exact. My grams never speaks to me without saying my full name like I'm important or in trouble. I never know. Her tone is always the same. Everyone else calls me Rosie—well, almost everyone. My mother just calls me Rose. And no, it isn't a family name, although it's what I tell everyone. The real story is a bit embarrassing.

She named me after a character on her favorite eighties television show, The Golden Girls. Yep, the one that thanks you for being a friend in its memorable opening sequence. You guessed it; I'm named after the semi-old woman who is ditzy yet smart, clumsy yet coordinated, and utterly naive. A prediction of her future daughter because she couldn't have thought of a more suitable name for me. Except for the old part, I'm all of those things. I admit it. Maybe it's better to say I accept it. I'm klutzy, gullible, and insanely scattered. Organized chaos is what I call it. It's the reason I'm twenty-six and alone. At least that's what Michael told me when he left.

Grams once told me that there are five pivotal moments in a person's life, and it's our responsibility to recognize what they are and where we allow them to lead us. She is right. I can tell you the moments that changed me and, well, where they lead me. I once thought Michael leaving me had been the most important, life-altering moment of my life. I was wrong. I guess we'll see where they lead me because I, Rosie Fisher, move through life like I'm running with a blindfold on and no map.

I'll just ignore the nagging little voice in my head telling me it's only inevitable before I run smack into trouble and land flat on my ass.

The Beginning

Pivotal moment number one

happened one rainy day...

CHAPTER One

S tanding outside my office building under the awning, I huff out a breath as I watch quarter-sized raindrops fall from the dark, foggy sky. It's on rainy days like this I wonder why I prayed to end the drought we've been having for years now. I should be relieved, but the idea of El Nino isn't all that appealing. Of course, I didn't bring an umbrella or a raincoat or any appropriate clothing for wet weather. I can hear my mother now: *This is why you need to watch the news, Rose. It keeps you informed.*

I hate the news. It only depresses me, and frankly, I don't need to watch the news to know that bad things are happening in our world. I don't need to hear about the evil that goes on around me. I choose to live in my little bubble. I just wish my bubble protected me from the sudden change in weather patterns, too.

Looking up at the dark sky again, I curse my insane addiction to caffeine. The Roasting Company is only around the corner; it's possible I can make a run for it with little damage. My red pea coat will surely protect my white top and me from looking like I'm a contestant in a wet t-shirt contest. I'm doing it.

Although it's buttoned, I pull my jacket closed around my neck and took my chances with the rain.

Dashing across the street and around the corner, toward the warm haven of The Roasting Company Coffee House, my hopes of making it to shelter only marginally wet have been, quite literally, doused. I can feel my pea coat grow laden with moisture. In other words, I'm drenched.

I can see the door up ahead, calling my name to hurry, to offer me sanctuary from the rain. The brick exterior of the building is looking redder from the water coating it. I love the way it looks, but I'd love it more if I were warm and dry.

Deciding to run a little faster, I ignore the dangers of wearing slick-soled flats on the wet ground.

Just as I reach the entrance, I put my hand out to open the front door. But my hand never makes it. In fact, I'm pretty sure my feet reach the door first as they go flying out from under me. This moment feels like I'm in slow motion, and there's nothing I can do to stop it. With typical Rosie flare, I'm about to land flat on my wet back. I squeeze my eyes shut as I brace myself for impact with the concrete below me.

Releasing a quiet, delayed scream, I anticipate the pain I will surely feel. I land hard, against the soft but firm chest of someone, my head cradled in the crook of their arm, my eyes still squeezed tightly closed. Slow motion. The world around me is still going in slow motion, silent around me. That annoying inner voice is back again, whispering, *Open your eyes, Rosie. Face your inescapable embarrassment.*

Slowly, I open my eyelids and blink. My caramel eyes are finally looking up into my savior's crystal-blue. My face immediately deepens to a dark crimson that travels down to my chest.

A concerned look on his face, his raspy voice whispering across my skin, he asks, "Are you alright?"

My gaze remains locked on his; I smile brightly. "Of course, better than alright. Normally, I would be on the ground right now, even wetter than I already am. But, um…do you mind letting me go so I can stand up?"

His lips turn up in one corner, giving me a crooked smile.

It says I'm awkward yet cute. *Typical,* I think as he helps me stand upright and opens the door.

"Shall we?" he asks, still smiling.

"Yes, thank you again," I reply, smiling back.

The warmth of the room and the strong smell of freshly brewed coffee hit me. I love it. Moving my way towards the end of the line, I wipe the drops of rain from my face. I can still feel the heaviness of my drenched coat. I pull my long, chocolate-colored locks from my face. I'm sure I look like a drowned rat, but it will be worth it. Because coffee. It's everything.

"Those shoes aren't made for running, especially in the rain," deep voice states from behind me.

I swing around so quickly; I knock into the same guy who kept me from falling only moments ago. He stumbles back a little, taken off guard, raising his hands to grab my forearms.

"Whoa, careful. I didn't mean to startle you." He grins.

I laugh. I laugh? Shit, awkward moment number two. I press my lips together. The smirk remains in place on his face.

"I'm Andrew Nallen," he informs me, reaching his hand out in my direction.

Staring first at his large hand then up to his ruggedly handsome face, my cheeks color once again before I blurt out, "I'm Rose Fisher, most people call me Rosie."

His expression doesn't change, but I swear his eyes twinkle.

Taking my small hand, he suggests, "You can call me Drew. It's what everyone but my mom calls me."

This time, I smile. "Well, pleased to meet you, Drew. Thank you again for rescuing me from total embarrassment."

"You're very welcome." He laughs.

I hear a familiar voice from behind the counter call my name. Turning, I beam at Andy standing behind the counter. Andrew? They have the same name. I almost laugh out loud, but stop myself when I realize I would be laughing alone. I don't need any more awkward moments this morning.

"Hello, Rosie. The usual?" he greets me in his charming British accent.

"Hi, Andy. Please, and thank you," I reply, moving closer to the counter.

"You got it," he answers then places his attention on the person behind me. "What about you, Drew? What will it be today?"

Andy seems to be familiar with Drew. I turn my head to get a good look at his face again. Have I seen him in here before? I'm here every day, and I don't think I've seen him. My mom's voice creeps into my thoughts again. *"Rose, honey, you need to pay better attention to the world around you. You might miss something important."* Not that Drew is important, but if Andy knows his name, then he is in here often. I just don't recall seeing him. Ever. He's handsome. More than handsome, actually, and I should've noticed him without needing to fall into his arms first.

"Let's get crazy today, Andy. I'll take a black coffee. Iced."

Yuck, black coffee, I think.

Damn. There's that smirk again. His eyes dart to mine, and his smile widens. I turn away from him and back to Andy to pay him for my coffee. I feel the heat in my cheeks again. I'm pathetic. I want to laugh again. *Walk away, Rosie. Walk. A. Way.*

Andy hands my change and coffee to me. "Thanks, sweetie. Stay dry...well, don't get any more wet than you already are now," he says, a humorous look on his face.

Pushing my hair off of my face again, I assure him I won't.

Before I walk away, I politely turn to Drew, who is standing behind me in line. "Drew, thanks again. Maybe I'll see you around."

"I'm sure you will. Bye, Rosie, and no more running in those shoes. I won't always be there to catch you," he jokes.

Walking away, I stop and look back one last time. His back is to me, chatting with Andy. Admittedly, I would have noticed him if we'd both been in here at the same time before. Or would I have? I turn back to the door and stare through the glass outside. It's still dark and dreary outside but thank god it has stopped raining.

When I get back into the office, I look up just in time to see Abbey brightly shining as she walks toward me. "Good morning! I can't wait for you to read this new ar…tic…le.

Her expression completely changes as soon as she is standing in front of me. I know that look; she is disappointed about something.

"Seriously, Rosie. Do you even own a mirror? I mean, when you wake up and put on your clothes in the morning, are your eyes open?" Abbey laughs, but there is a bit of stress behind her words. She takes my coffee out of my hand and places it on my desk before taking me by the arm and marching me into the ladies' room. "You're a successful copy editor. It's crucial you dress the part. I love you, but really, Rosie."

"What are you doing, Abbey?"

Without answering me, she rolls her eyes and turns me toward the mirror. "Look at yourself, Rosie. You're one hot mess." She throws her hands up in exasperation. "I guess it could be worse. It's still early, so your interaction with people who have eyes has been limited."

I stare at my reflection. I look like a wet rat. Or worse. My hair is lying in wet clumps against my head and face. My skirt is a little crooked, the seam nearly down the center instead of on my sides. The worst part is my cardigan sweater looks as if a kindergartener buttoned it. It's lopsided, and all the buttons are in the wrong holes. Abbey's right, I'm a mess. My appearance could've been mortifying if…

"Oh, shit," I say, so loud I startle Abbey.

She looks at my face and rolls her eyes. "My God, Rosie. What happened?"

Turning toward her, I give her a bright smile. "Well, let's see. I may or may not have slipped while running through the rain when I went to get coffee. And I may or may not have fallen into the arms of a handsome stranger."

Abbey begins rubbing her temples, looks at me and turns to leave the bathroom. "Only you, Rosie. Only you." A giggle slips out as she leaves the bathroom.

I'm left standing alone, staring after her and contemplating on a scale of one to ten just how likely it is that I will see Drew again in the future. Except, what does it matter? I'm not interested in worrying about what a handsome stranger thinks. I just need to worry about me.

CHAPTER Two

A pparently, the chances are good. Like *ten on a scale from one to ten* good. Because I just walked into the coffee house and immediately spotted Drew quietly sitting across the room at a corner table.

I look up at the ceiling and stick my tongue out. *Thanks, God,* I think.

Looking back in the direction Drew is sitting, I study his features. His head is down, the sunlight filtering through the windows shining over him, highlighting the red in his dark hair. Broad shoulders. Olive skin. Even though he's sitting down, I can tell his body is lean due to the tight-fitting burgundy T-shirt he is wearing. How did I not notice him before the other day?

"Rosie's in the house, Andy!" I hear a familiar voice yell behind me.

I freeze as all eyes in the coffee shop focus on me, including an amused pair of green that just so happen to belong to the very body I'm admiring. His mouth quirks up in one corner. Not knowing what to do, I lift my hand in a shy wave and quickly turn toward my friend, Lynn—the one who just announced me only moments ago.

Before I greet Lynn, I hear Andy call out a hello to me from behind the counter.

"Good Morning, Lynn. How's it going?" I ask with a smile on my face. I lean down to give him a hug. Lynn is probably in his fifties, handsome, and friendly. He spends his days in and out of the shop, and every morning when I come in, if he's here, Lynn announces me. In fact, he greets nearly every person who walks through the door. I've seen him make more people smile than I can count.

"I'm better now that you're here," he says in innocent flirtation.

"Well, my morning is better now that I've seen you, too," I tell him.

Suddenly, I feel someone standing close to my side. "What about me?" a male voice asks, joining our conversation. Turning toward him, I'm surprised to see Drew standing there. He still has that crooked smile on his face. Now that he's closer, I can see specks of gold in his blue eyes and for a moment, I'm mesmerized into silence.

My gaze travels down from his eyes to his perfectly shaped lips. When they pull into a wide grin, I snap out of my trance and turn a deep shade of crimson.

Oh, shit. I'm about to say something stupid. I know it because that's what I always do when I'm embarrassed. And right now, I'm definitely embarrassed.

Look in his eyes, Rosie. It shows confidence. Look. Into. His. Eyes.

So I do, and it's almost like he knows I'm about to say something I'm going to regret too. It's something in the way he's watching me.

"Yes!" I shout with a little too much enthusiasm. I sigh, taking a moment to compose myself. Pushing an errant strand of hair behind my ear, I bite my bottom lip before saying, "I mean, yes. It's nice to see you too…again…also, Drew."

Jesus, Rosie, you were an English major. Get it together. You know how to speak.

Ugh, there's that lip quirk again. It makes me want to lick them.

Is it hot in here? Damn it; my mind is running rampant. Stop. It.

His lips catch my attention again. They're pretty. So nice and perfectly shaped. Dreamy.

"Good, I was hoping you'd say that. Do you have time to sit a while?" he asks me. My eyes snap up from his mouth, and I blink a few times until they focus on his. "So? What do ya say?" Waiting for my answer, his eyes never leave mine.

It's intense, and the weight of his stare begins to bend me. I don't want to be bent. I've been bent before by a charming, handsome man. At this moment, something in me resists the urge to cower away from his offer, which is something I might typically do. It took Michael months to get me to relax around him. Abbey whispers, *You can do it, Rosie.*

Yes, I can do it. I'm in charge, and I want to sit down with this man. This breathtaking and confident man. Take a chance, Rosie. There's a shift in me. I want to try something different. Be something different.

Straightening my shoulders, I stand a bit taller. "Sure, I think I'd like that," I tell him.

His eyebrow lifts over one eye. "You think?"

Just then, the old me of one minute ago, the less poised version, almost lets his teasing get to her. Instead, I never miss a beat.

Lifting my chin, I look him directly in the eyes. "Yes, I think. We'll have to see if you can make it worth my while."

A burst of laughter escapes him, and his eyes crinkle in the corners and dimples form perfectly on either side of his mouth. *Breathtaking* is certainly the right word to use when describing him, because I just lost mine.

Taking my hand, he leads me to his table. "You're adorable."

At first, I feel a sense of outrage that he called me adorable. That he sees what everyone else sees. Plain, adorable, silly Rosie. But it quickly dissipates because I can only think about my hand in his, our skin touching, the warmth of his palm against my cool one.

Normally, I would run out the door, but I vow to be different. To be more vibrant. To be more noticeable. To just be more.

We've been sitting here at a little corner table for five minutes now. I've been giving Drew one-word answers to nearly everything he has asked me. The old Rosie and the new self-proclaimed confident Rosie are about to come to blows within me. I can feel it, and it's not going to be pretty.

I continue to watch him as he talks. Drew is different. I knew it the moment I looked up at his face when he kept me from landing on my wet behind. He is self-assured and comfortable in his skin. He is effortlessly put together. His eyes glowed with charm then, just as they are at this moment. I'm jealous. I feel seduced every time he glances my way. He exudes a boldness I didn't know I wanted until I saw him again today. I want it for myself. I don't just want it; I need it, and I've got to find a way to have it.

"Well, this is the first," he says, interrupting my thoughts.

Blinking at him, I look up to find his eyes sparkling with humor. "I'm sorry, the first what?" I ask, thankful I actually heard what he said because I wasn't paying attention.

His smile goes crooked again. "The first time I've bored a woman into silence," he replies, an amused lilt to his voice. "In fact, I'm not sure a woman has ever been bored with me." He looks perplexed for a brief moment, then the look disappears into what I assume is his usual poised look.

A blush runs through my cheeks and down my chest.

"I'm so sorry. You're not boring me; I'm a little preoccupied today," I tell him, but of course, I leave out the part about just what is on my mind.

"Good, I was beginning to worry," he says, but he doesn't look worried at all. "So, why haven't I seen you before a week ago, Rosie Fisher?"

I blush again, twisting a loose strand of hair around my finger. It's a nervous habit my mother has been trying to break me of for years. Obviously, it has yet to work.

"I was wondering the same thing the other day," I confess. "I'm here all the time."

He smiles. "Well, we know one another now. I guess that's all that matters."

"Yep. It seems so," I say, smiling back. I sound ridiculous. Although I can't see the grin I currently have plastered on my face, I know it looks forced. I'm sure it says, *I'm an idiot who can't carry on a normal conversation.*

Get a grip, Rosie. Jesus.

I'm not sure why I do this when I get around guys or people in general. I guess it's me.

As I watch Drew's face light up again, I'm struck by the idea once more that I want to be different. I want to change and be someone different. Someone new. I finally see what Michael meant when he told me he wanted someone with more confidence. I just need to figure out how I'm going to do it.

CHAPTER Three

Over the last two weeks, I've seen Drew on several occasions. Each time, he invites me to sit with him, and he chats away while I observe his every move. He talks but never reveals too much about himself. It's usually meaningless chatter, which is fine. I can see he puts up walls and does it so flawlessly that he makes you feel like he is giving you a part of himself he isn't sharing with anyone else. I find it fascinating.

Of course, I interact with him some and with very little grace, as you can imagine. All the while, I daydream of how I just might be able to change into the smooth, collected person he seems to be.

Today isn't any different. He's talking, and I'm watching the way he moves through our conversation with ease. Thinking. Taking it all in and still coming up with nothing. I really need to find help, but I'm trying to avoid the embarrassment of telling someone that I don't like who I am. That I want to be different. My family would roll their eyes. Abbey? Maybe? A little excitement runs through me when Abbey's voice pops in my head. She will get it. In fact, I'm pretty sure she will encourage it. Yes! Abbey! My face is hurting because my lips have spread so tight across my face. I let out a small snort. Sometimes I'm so clueless; why didn't I think of her before?

I hear a throat clearing across the table from me. *Shit. I did it again.*

"There you go again," he says in mock seriousness. "You're really beginning to hurt my feelings."

"Oh, give me a break," I tell him, rolling my eyes to avoid looking directly into his electric-blue. I noticed earlier, the flecks of gold I've seen before aren't there. It doesn't matter. They're mesmerizing and beautiful regardless.

He barks in laughter. It's a pleasant sound. Even his laugh sounds unflappable. It hits me just as it has a dozen times over the last three weeks I've been around Drew; he is way out of my league. I may not have learned much about him personally, but that I have figured out.

"Tell me something," he states, suddenly becoming a little more serious. "Out of all the times we've sat here, you've hardly told me anything about you. I can't figure you out. I know what I see, but I have no idea what you think about almost anything." He leans forward and rests his chin in his hand. *Feeling's mutual,* I think. Before I can respond, he continues, "Well, except black coffee. I know you hate black coffee."

This time, I'm the one who lets out a loud, very unladylike cackle. I cover my mouth quickly as my eyes widen in embarrassment.

"You're adorable, Rosie Fisher." He laughs.

Adorable. I really hate that word. *Adorable.* Ugh. Someone kill me now, because if I have to hear a guy call me adorable one more time, I think I may go crazy. I hate adorable.

"See!" he exclaims. "Why that face?"

I scrunch my nose up at him. "What face?" I ask.

He points at me, a huge grin on his face like he just won a prize. "That one!" He laughs. " I called you adorable, and you made that face like you're disgusted. You have to tell me why."

I don't know if I want to tell him why. He must notice my reluctance because he says, "Okay, let's do this." I look at him skeptically. His smile widens. "We'll take turns asking one another questions, and we must answer it and answer it truthfully. Deal?"

I'm not sure how comfortable I am with this, but I nod anyway.

"Okay, since I'm putting you on the spot and this was my idea, you get to ask the first question," he suggests.

What do I ask him? I watch as he tries to keep his face neutral while I stare him down and contemplate what I will ask Drew. I could use this little game to my advantage so I can ask him anything I want without coming across as a weirdo.

Tapping my finger to my chin like I'm thinking, I allow the questions to spin in my brain like a wheel. I'll keep it safe and impersonal to start. "Okay, what do you do for a living?"

A deep belly laughs echoes around us, but he quickly recovers. "Really, that's the first thing you want to know?"

I scowl at him, and he puts his hands up in defense of the annoyance I just aimed at him.

"Okay…okay…well, I'm a graphic designer for a startup company in San Jose, but I work from home. I'm pretty lucky because I get to make my own hours," he tells me. I can hear a bit of pride in his voice. "My turn, and I'll cut you some slack by asking the same question. What does Rosie Fisher do for work?"

My face lights up. This topic of conversation is my element. I love my job; it's the one thing I'm confident of in my life. "I like that face…that's a nice look on you," he states so sincerely. At first, I'm confused by what he means by what he just said. I look at him and smile, but my confusion remains in my eyes. His face turns serious, but there is humor behind his features. "Your smile. It transforms you. You're pretty, but when you smile like you did just now, you're something spectacular."

My eyes go wide, and the smile I'm wearing disappears. My face heats, and I start rubbing on my chest because those damn anxiety butterflies are fluttering around. He called me spectacular. Not beautiful or anything plain. Drew Nallen just called me spectacular.

A normal person would say thank you. I'm not typical.

Instead, I giggle and blurt out, "You're so full of shit!"

"What? Most people would say thank you," he says, a bemused grin on his face.

"I'm sorry," I tell him shyly. "I tend to say what's on my mind. Thank you, even if it's a ridiculous thing to say."

'Well, now I know you're horrible at accepting a compliment, but I still don't know what you do for a living," he teases. He moves on from my protest of his compliment and waits for me to answer him.

"I'm a copy editor for the local paper," I answer him finally.

"Nice. I'm going to assume from your spectacular smile—" he pauses and holds his hand up when I start to protest again "—the smile is because you love your job."

Nodding my head, I smile again because I can't help myself. This time, I'm not sure if it's because I'm talking about work or because of Drew. Either way, it doesn't really matter.

"Your turn," he reminds me after a moment of silence.

Ah, yes. My turn. What do I want to know about Drew Nallen now?

"Do you have a girlfriend, or are you dating?" I feel myself turn red when the question leaves my mouth.

Drew looks a little surprised by the question, but I can tell he is trying to figure out the best way to answer this question. Taking a deep breath, he says, "No girlfriend. I don't do girlfriends anymore. I'm what you call a serial dater. I date. A lot. No attachments make life less complicated, and it's easier on the heart."

I wait for him to continue because it looks like he might have more to say, but he doesn't. His eyes cloud over with this distant look before he snaps out of it. He asks me his next question, and this begins our back-and-forth game for the next thirty minutes, learning as much as we can about one another. I've never felt so open and comfortable in my entire adult life.

I glance down at my watch and realize I need to get back to work because I only have ten minutes left of my lunch break. Where did the time go? Drew notices and says, "Thanks for spending your lunch with me. I like you, Rosie Fisher."

It's funny, but I'm suddenly struck by the fact that I really like Drew, too. "I like you too, Drew."

We both stand, and he waves goodbye to me as I walk away. I turn back one last time, and I know I can be anyone I want to be.

Walking into the office like a woman on a mission, I take long strides toward Abbey's desk. She looks up just as I reach her. Her expression transforms into one of concern.

"What's wrong?" she asks me as she stands up.

"I need your help," I tell her. "I don't know what happened, Abbey," I continue as I begin pacing around her desk. "One minute I was fine being me, the girl who is messy and awkward. The girl who had her heart broken. Then I met him, and I want to be something different." I'm speaking so quickly I'm not even giving her time to respond. "Not that I want him. God, it would be nice to capture the attention of someone like Drew Nallen, but I'm not stupid. It's not like I can suddenly morph into Kate Upton. I'm a little more realistic than that. I want to be an improved version of myself. Not for Michael. Not for a guy like Drew, but for me. Me, Rose Marie Fisher."

Finally taking a breath, I stop and face a silent Abbey. She regards me with an unsure look on her face. If I'm honest, that's not unusual, but there is something different about the way her brown eyes haven't left my face.

Suddenly, she's throwing her hands in the air, and she releases a long, drawn-out sigh. "What in the ever-loving hell are you talking about, Rosie?" She sounds exasperated, adding a dramatic flair to her tone. "You want to change! Are you insane?" Her eyes look a little wild. I take a small step back.

Walking around her desk, Abbey stands in front of me now, wiping a cookie crumb from my cheek I didn't even realize was there. Crap. I'm not sure if she realizes it or not, but Abbey is just as crazy as I am. Her breathing slows, and she says, "Okay, sorry. I just got off a really awful phone call, and your ramblings sent me over the edge. Did you just ask me to help you change?"

Part of me wants to laugh at her because as ridiculous as she thinks I am, she is too. I mean, why else would she be my best friend?

We're different. We each have our own quirks, but the one thing that separates us is exactly what I need. Abbey De Diego is the most put-together, self-assured person I know.

Pushing my shoulders back, I smile my most brilliant smile. "Yes, that's exactly what I'm asking you."

She walks over to me, putting her arms around me and squeezing me so tight I feel like my insides might break, then she releases me. "Oh, Rosie. You're so cute." I hate the tone of her voice. It's the one she uses when she think she knows me better than I know myself. Sometimes when she talks to me this way, I imagine her patting me on the top of my head like I'm a little toy Yorkie. "I've been trying to get you to do this for years. I've tried, and I've tried, until I finally convinced myself it's a hopeless cause. You, my friend, are exactly who you are, and it's what I love about you. You don't need to change. You just need to get laid."

Staring at the giddy look on her face, my mouth falls open. I am beginning to feel uncomfortable with this conversation. Laid? How does she always manage to highjack my plans and change my entire course?

"I need to get laid," I repeat out loud.

Putting her hand on her hip, Abbey laughs. "That's what I just said. You need to get out there. Experience life. Have no-strings-attached sex." She pauses, a serious look on her face, then continues, "Safe, of course."

Nodding, I agree with her. "You're right. I'm silly." I place another smile on my face, trying to wrap my mind around how she can think this is even remotely a good idea. "Thank you for keeping me from embarrassing myself. I'll just go out and get laid." Sarcasm drips from every word.

"I love you, Rosie. You're perfect the way you are, even if I give you shit all the time for being a mess," Abbey says sincerely. I know she means well. I know she wants what's best for me. But she doesn't realize that I'm tired of floating through life. I want a plan. I want more. And I'm going to figure out a way to be bolder—to be more. "Although, you could make sure you look in the mirror before you leave the house a little more often," she says jokingly. I laugh because coming from anyone else that would be an insult, but Abbey loves clothes. She loves makeup and always looks impeccable. She honestly is trying to help.

"You're crazy, do you know that? We're talking about me, Abbey. The girl whose fiancé broke off their engagement and ended their four-year relationship because she is boring, prudish, and not adventurous enough. That's me," I remind her.

"That's bullshit, Rosie, and you know it," she protests. "Michael is a dick. He doesn't know what he had, and frankly, he's the one who made you boring. He never knew you. He held you back, and it's time for you to act like the Rosie I know and love."

Abbey had once again begun pacing around me, but she is now stopped directly in front of me. Placing her hands on my shoulders, she smiles wide. "Rosie, I demand you date casually without expectations. Take your time. Be happy. Have fun because you deserve it."

She's right. This is exactly what I need, and screw Michael.

"You're right. I'm doing it," I declare. Abbey throws her fist in the air in triumph, then I'm struck with nerves. My eyes widen with fear. "Wait! How am I going to do this?"

A smile spreads across her face, and she bats her eyelashes.

"Match.com? The old school way…in a bar?" she suggests gleefully.

Rolling my eyes, I hope I don't regret bringing Abbey into this plan.

When I walk into The Roasting Company the next afternoon, I nearly trip when I spot Drew sitting with a tall, thin blonde. It's the first time I've seen him in here with someone else.

I feel a little ache in the pit of my stomach, but quickly will it away.

"Who are you staring at?" Abbey asks me as we sit down at one of the small tables against the front windows.

Looking up at her, I frown. "I wasn't staring," I hiss quietly.

"Uh huh, you were totally staring," she argues.

"Whatever, I wasn't staring. I just happened to notice Drew," I maintain, taking a sip of my mocha.

Abbey turns her head to look in the direction I've been looking as we sit down. "Abbey!" I say in quiet exasperation. She whips back around almost immediately, a wide grin on her face. I can see something in her eyes I don't think I like. It's strange how I can know what she thinks before she even tells me. "Oh no, it's not happening," I insist.

"Why not?" she whines.

"Because!" I shout a little too loudly, my gaze shifting to where Drew is sitting. Damn it; he sees me now because he's lifting his hand in a wave. I respond in kind. Turning back to Abbey, I notice her eyes on me, shining with a giddiness she has no right to feel. "No, I can't. It's Drew. He told me himself. He's a serial dater. No commitment," I explain.

She's making me nervous because her expression hasn't changed.

"Rosie, you just described the perfect guy for what you're looking for..." Abbey tells me before I interrupt her.

"No, I didn't because it's Drew," I insist.

"What's Drew? Well, other than me," a deep voice says from behind me.

I freeze in my chair. Abbey must see the look on my face because she quickly stands and throws her hand practically in Drew's face. "Hi, I'm Abbey, Rosie's best friend. You must be Drew. She's told me so much about you."

"Hey, Abbey. Rosie told me about you the other day," he replies. I'm assuming he shook her hand because I still haven't turned to look at him. He places his hand on my shoulder in a gentle touch. "Hey, Rosie," he says.

Slowly, I turn in my chair so I can see his face. He's shining just as he always does. "Hi," I respond, my voice low.

Abbey is taking her seat again when she asks him, "Would you like to join us, Drew?"

He looks down at me as if he's waiting for my approval, so I nod. "Sure" he replies.

Drew pulls a chair from the empty table next to us. "So what's happening, ladies?

I remain silent, but what does it matter when Abbey is around? She's a great buffer. I just hope she doesn't embarrass me.

"Not much, taking a little afternoon break from work. What about you?" Abbey carries the conversation.

"Had a little lunch date before I head back to work," he reveals.

Abbey's raises her eyebrow at me. I'm going to kill her. I need to say something before he wonders why I'm not talking. Find your voice, Rosie. Jesus.

"How's the project you told me about going?" I ask, feeling good about my ability to say anything at all, especially something coherent.

"It's good. I actually need to get going soon because I need to be finished by tomorrow afternoon," he answers. I notice again just as I did yesterday the way his eyes light up when he talks about his work.

"We actually need to get going too," I say, standing up. Both Abbey and Drew look at me, but follow my cue and stand also.

I don't know why I'm acting like such a Nervous Nellie. I like Drew. I don't feel uncomfortable with him, but I do feel out of my element today. I think it's the whole situation with this casual dating thing and Abbey's suggestion I try it out on Drew.

Just when I'm about to reach for my coat hanging on the back of the chair, Drew takes it off before I do. "Let me help you, turn around," he instructs me, his voice tender.

I look into his eyes then slowly turn, catching a glimpse of Abbey's face as I look away from them. She looks a bit shocked and intrigued at the same time. Drew holds my coat out so I can place my arms in it.

"Thank you," I say politely.

As I turn, I pull the hair from out of my coat, smiling when I face Drew.

"You're welcome," he replies, a shy smile on his face.

We all head to the door together; Drew holds the door as Abbey and I walk through it. I realize that's two things he's done to indicate how gentlemanly he is in the last few minutes. It brings to mind Drew is a complete contradiction to the persona he says he plays, which is a playboy.

When we say our goodbyes again, I watch Drew disappear around the corner. There is definitely more to Drew Nallen than he lets on, and I like him.

The Arrangement

Pivotal moment number two happened in a bar.

When I made a deal I believed I could handle.

CHAPTER *Four*

I'm sitting at the bar of the swanky new restaurant on Pacific Avenue, taking a bite out of a vodka-soaked olive, staring at the door. Abbey and I were on a mission tonight: go out and find me my very own Ashton Kutcher from *No Strings Attached* minus the eventually-fall-in-love part. The only problem is Abbey went to the bathroom thirty minutes ago, and now I'm sitting alone because she found herself her own handsome conquest. I pop another olive in my mouth, savoring the saltiness before downing the rest of my martini.

I don't need Abbey's help. I'm a smart, twenty-seven-year-old woman who is more than capable of finding myself a man. I wave at the bartender, and he nods, holding his finger up to signal he will be with me in a moment. I just need a brilliant plan.

As I tap my finger to my chin, my mind runs wild with ideas of how and what I need to do to be the new, adventurous me.

Aha! That's it! I'll just sit here at this bar, and the next guy to walk in will be my adventure. As soon as the thought crosses my mind, he walks in.

He, as in the stranger of my dreams. Tall, dark, handsome, and a great dresser. He's per—ewww! No! Tall, dark, and handsome just picked his nose. In public. He actually stuck his finger in his nose, pulled it out, and looked at it. Who does that after the age of eight? The dream just turned into a nightmare. I frown.

Let's move on and try this again.

During the booger debacle, another guy walked up to the opposite end of the bar, but his back is to me. It is a lean and defined back if the tight fitting shirt is any indication. He has a full head of hair, and it looks nice. I lift the martini the bartender just placed in front of me to my mouth, and as it wets my lips, Mr. Nice From Behind turns to face me. His head isn't the only part of his body that's full of hair. He has hair peeking from beneath his button-down shirt, except he seems to have missed several buttonholes because his gorilla chest is showing. And what the hell is up with the thick gold chains hanging around his neck? Oh damn, he just caught me staring, and he winked at me, throwing a cheesy grin on the side. This whole situation just became worse than the booger guy. No, dude. No. I quickly turn my head, dropping it onto the bar.

Jesus, is this what I have to work with? I may be a bit off my game, but I'm not that desperate. Maybe tonight isn't going to be my night. I'll even admit I may need Abbey's help. Or maybe this is hopeless and I need to call it a night. I mean, who am I kidding? How am I going to do this? I can't even remember how to act with a guy who isn't Michael. Once upon a time he liked my quirky personality. My awkwardness. He said it was cute. Adorable. He's the reason I hate being called those things now. According to Michael, all the things he once loved weren't so adorable any longer; he wanted something different.

As I lift my head and take another sip from my martini, thinking of calling it a night, he walks through the door.

Drew Nallen.

The very guy who put this whole idea in motion, even if he doesn't know it.

"Maybe he'll do it," Abbey is suddenly whispering in my ear.

I shake my head. "Wait, what? No. No, he wouldn't," I insist.

She stands next to me; we watch Drew as he speaks with the hostess. The blonde is giggling and batting her eyelashes at him. He acts as if he's paying attention to her, but his eyes tell a different story that even I can see from this distance.

"How do you know he wouldn't?" Abbey asks me, never taking her eyes off of him.

"I know because that is Drew," I inform her as if that simple statement should explain it all.

"Yes, I'm aware. Drew, the guy from The Roasting Company." The sanguine tone in her voice makes me nervous.

"The one and only," I state, a bit of longing in my voice. "Drew, the guy who isn't relationship material.

Her eyes finally leave him and focus on me. I can tell the wheels are turning in her head, and the look of determination on her face is one I've seen time and time again.

"No, Abbey. You—" I try to plead before she interrupts me.

"Rosie Fisher, this is your man. This isn't about a relationship, and you need to remember that because you're the one who decided this is what you wanted. He's got the confidence and charm. He's used to this kind of relationship. You've told me over and over he dates but never commits. All you need to do is be honest and ask him for what you want." She glances back at him just as he begins to make his way in our direction. "Rosie, he's the one. Now ask. I'm going back to Hottie McHotstuff I met on my way out of the bathroom. I'll call you tomorrow."

She leans forward and places a kiss on my cheek, then lifts her hand in a modestly flirtatious way in Drew's direction.

I look up just in time for my eyes to lock with Drew's. He smiles like it was his intention to meet me here all along. When the warmth of his smile reaches me, I know I'm about to ask Drew Nallen to be my friend with benefits. Forget Ashton Kutcher; Drew is going to be my Justin Timberlake. I lift my hand in a small wave; it's shaking, so I pull it back down quickly.

What are the odds this will work? He's probably going to think I've lost my mind. Because really, what does Drew know about me?

I begin to list them off in my head. He knows I'm a twenty-seven-year-old copy editor for the local paper. I live alone. He knows I have three siblings who all live in Texas, where I grew up. He knows my best friend is Abbey. Drew has asked me all of these tiny yet personal details about myself. This won't work.

Tapping my fingernails against the bar as I wait for him to reach me, my nerves are beginning to get the best of me.

What am I thinking? How can I think this is a good idea? I'm a lunatic! He's going to think I'm a floozy! Just when I contemplate getting up and walking out of here, Drew waltzes up to my side with his usual swagger.

He smiles wider, a genuine smile that lights up his face. I reciprocate, listing everything I know about him off in my head.

He's a graphic designer. He lives alone. He has one sister and three brothers. His parents are still happily married. He grew up here in Santa Cruz. He likes to surf in his free time, which would explain his well-sculpted body and sun-kissed skin. He has kind eyes. He laughs a lot. The best part is he seems to honestly enjoy my company.

Just as this thought enters my mind, Drew takes the seat across from me. "I'm glad I saw you over here," he tells me as he reaches over and pulls one of the olives from my drink off the toothpick with his teeth. I watch him without saying a word when he immediately pops another into his mouth and grins. He's comfortable; that's good. "So what's up?" he asks me when he finishes chewing. He reaches for my drink again; I slap his hand but he takes the drink anyway. He laughs before continuing, "Are you here with someone?"

Pushing the strands of hair behind my ears that have come loose from the messy bun I tied high on my head, I close my eyes for a moment, silently chanting, *I can do this...I can do this.* When I open my eyes again, Drew is watching me with a curious look on his handsome face.

Taking a deep breath, I blurt out, "I want you to teach me."

His eyebrows shoot up. "You want me to teach you?"

"No! I mean, yes, but no," I try to explain. "Damn it; I'm nervous."

Drew takes me completely off guard when he reaches his hand across the table and lays it over mine. His lips curve up in one corner. Man, he's smooth. Immediately, a calm washes over me. I want this, and suddenly, now more than ever, I'm confident he's the one who can help me.

"I want you to help me. You have experience with…things," I mumble, eyes wide. I want him to understand what I'm trying to say, but he's going to make me explain it. I can tell I've completely mystified him. Drew thought he had me figured out, and I've thrown him for a loop. Good.

"I know things? You want me to teach you…things? What kind of things, Rosie?" he questions me.

A blush colors my cheeks. Nodding my head, I admit, "Yes, you're experienced. Things that I want to be better at, more sure about."

"Things," he states, a light shining in his eyes that wasn't there before.

"Yes," I return, straightening in my chair and pushing my shoulders back.

He rests his elbow on the bar and begins tapping his lips with one finger, watching me silently as if he is trying to figure out an answer to a difficult puzzle.

"Things," I say, unable to remain silent under his scrutiny any longer. He smiles. My blood boils. He's laughing at me. Abruptly, I stand. "Forget it," I huff out and turn to walk away.

He wraps his hands firmly around my wrist, and I freeze. I can't bring myself to look back; my head falls, and I focus on the way his large fingers press into my skin. Surely he can feel my pulse speed up. Sometimes he makes me so damn nervous.

"I want you to say it, Rosie. Say the words." His voice is practically a whisper. Although he's still seated, it's as if I can feel his breath on my neck. The air between us changed in an instant. I nod my head slowly; it's only then that Drew releases my wrist.

Slowly, I turn around, sitting next to him at the bar once more.

His acute gaze fixated on my face, he waits. I look down at my newly manicured nails, the electric-blue polish part of my attempt to be more daring. When I look back up, Drew is still focused solely on me, his cheek dimpled on one side. I can't help but return his good humor.

"Say it, Rosie," he says, a little more demanding this time.

"You're so confident and controlled. People are drawn to you. You demand attention when you walk in the door, and yet you're so amiable." I swallow the tiny lump that has lodged itself in my throat at the last thought in my head. Sighing, my next words come out in a hushed tone. "I have a feeling you're more capable of pleasing a woman than the average guy." His face lights up more and more with every word that leaves my mouth. My nerves are wound so tight; I begin to speak more quickly. "I want the same, and I want you to teach me. Because I like you and for some reason, I trust you." The last words come out in a low voice; I'm not sure he even heard me.

A temporary look of shock crosses his features before it disappears into something different altogether.

"I'm not sure if I knew what you were going to say, but that wasn't it," he admits, running a hand through his dark hair.

"I'm sorry," I blurt out. "You must think I'm insane."

He slides his hand and places it over mine lying on the bar. I look down and examine the way it swallows mine beneath it, shielding it in a protective way. It's this kind of touch that tells me he's so much more than the playboy he portrays himself to be. It's the reason I can trust him.

When he begins speaking again, I lift my gaze back up to his face.

"Rosie, I don't think you're insane, but I'm not exactly sure what you're proposing," he states, a serious look on his face.

Feeling a little indignant, I let my frustration seep into my tone. "I'm saying I want you to help me become a little bolder. I want you to show me how to attract a man and keep his interest without scaring him away."

He moves his hand away, running it through his hair, and I fight the urge to pull it back to mine.

Releasing a long, low sigh, Drew's eyes penetrate mine. "Are you sure you know what you're asking me? Because, Rosie, I'm not the nice guy. I'm not gentle, and I definitely don't commit. Shit, I really like you, but…"

He trails off, the look in his eyes begging me to understand why he's saying no to me and my proposition. It goes against his nature.

I laugh, and his expression twists into one of confusion.

"Drew, I know who you are. Sure, maybe we haven't been friends long, but I've seen you on a date, and from what you told me, you go through more girls in a month than most go through in a lifetime." This time, I place my hand over his and I'm still struck by the sheer size of his hand compared to mine. "I'm not asking you to date me in hopes it will lead to more. I'm asking you to spend some time with me, give me pointers, help me become a girl that can turn heads yet remain strong. I want this, and I want you to be the one to show me."

"You don't need me for this, Rosie. You deserve more than I can offer. Believe me when I say you deserve more than anything I can offer," he implores.

"I know what I'm asking. Drew, I know what I want, and I want it with you," I maintain.

The look on his face is the most serious I've ever seen. War is raging in the depths of his eyes. Worry. Excitement. More worry. Until I see the moment he makes his decision.

"Fine. I'll do this on one condition: you promise you won't have any expectations." I start to say something, but he continues, "And if you begin to feel differently, then you'll let me know, because I can't do more than casual, Rosie. You've also come to mean a lot to me, and I don't want to lose you."

"I understand. I don't want to lose your friendship, either," I confess. "I know who you are, and I want more than you can offer me long term. Don't worry," I say confidently, although a feeling of wary concern churns in the pit of my stomach.

As I watch his face, I think I see a brief shadow of disappointment cross his features at my words, but it quickly disappears, and I realize the thought is absurd. It's also one that would ignite a flame of desire for something Drew just made clear was not an option.

A silence lingers between us. He studies me, his eyes never leaving my face.

"Are you sure? No strings. No commitment," he states. The tone of his voice is telling me he wants to be firm in the stipulations of this arrangement I'm asking him to enter into with me.

Nodding, I repeat his words, "No strings. No commitments."

Drew gives me a slight nod and abruptly stands, holding his hand out to me.

As I take it, he jerks me up and into his embrace. I want to look around to see if anyone is watching us, but I can't take my eyes from his, and for one brief second, his gaze searches mine. Before I know what is happening, his lips are firmly against mine, coaxing my tight mouth to soften, and they do so without much effort. Drew Nallen is kissing me in the middle of the bar, and I'm kissing him back. I can feel his warmth. His control. I can feel my surrender, and it feels better than I could've imagined. Although intense, the kiss is short.

Drew pulls back, and when I open my eyes, he's staring at me with a surprised haze clouding his regard, then, as usual, his dimple appears on one side, and my insides melt.

"I'm sorry, but I think the pleasure of this situation is going to be all mine," I apologize.

His happy expression leaves his face. Shaking his head, Drew quietly scolds, "Lesson number one: never apologize or criticize yourself. It's the first rule of being more confident." Drew lifts one hand from my waist and places it lightly under my chin, shifting my gaze up to his. "Also, I fear your view on your capabilities is utterly skewed. I might be the one who will need to work harder on my pleasure skills."

I can't help myself; a smile lights up my face. I want to laugh. I want to argue, but instead, I accept his compliment as graciously as I can.

"So I'm supposed to be meeting some friends, but are you free for dinner tomorrow night?" Drew asks, still holding me in his arms as if we have done this a hundred times before today.

"Yes, tomorrow night is great. I get off work at five o'clock," I answer, trying to keep my voice steady. Being this close to him has my body electrified. I'm going to need to work on keeping myself in check.

As Drew leans in closer to me, I automatically tilt my face up to his, and he whispers, "I'll see you around seven. Text me your address." As the last word leaves his mouth, he places a soft, lingering kiss to my lips. Pulling back from our embrace, eyes shining, Drew smiles. "I'm going to like kissing you regularly, Rosie Fisher."

It was all so quick; I'm left staring after his departing figure, lips tingling and full of more hope than I thought possible. But it's that hopeful feeling that frightens me.

CHAPTER Five

I've spent most of the day tied up in knots. Abbey asked me at least a dozen times if I'm okay. And I nearly screamed, *No! I'm not okay, Abbey! I'm not because I asked Drew Nallen to show me how to be bolder and better at pleasing men! And he agreed! And...and...I'm not sure I can do casual. I promised him casual!* Instead, I remained silent and denied feeling anything but amazing.

She's excited. It's annoying, but it also makes me feel more eager for this little arrangement.

Now, I've just changed into my third outfit, and I have less than thirty minutes until Drew is supposed to be here. I wish I had accepted Abbey's offer to help me find something to wear. I would've saved myself from panic and time, but she would've made me feel even more anxiety overall. It is that reason alone I'm not letting her get too close.

I'm not sure how I let her make me think this is a good idea. I think about the person I am and the person I want to be. I want to be more than the girl everyone thinks I am. And more is exactly what I'll be with Drew's help.

I step in front of the mirror to inspect my reflection. My chocolate-brown hair is swept up perfectly in a loose bun. A few tendrils hang across my forehead. My strapless, spring-green dress perfectly complements my tawny skin and amber eyes. The way it hugs my curves makes me a little self-conscious, but I look…good. No, I look amazing. Like I've never looked before, and instantly, I know I've finally found the perfect outfit for my first date with Drew.

Yes, if I continue to step out of my comfort zone, and with Drew's help, I'll definitely find what I'm looking for at the end of this arrangement.

A wide smile slowly forms across my face. I'm practically unrecognizable, and I love it. This is the look I was going for tonight. I hope Drew likes it. The moment the thought crosses my mind, I frown, and before I can think too much about my mental slip, I hear a knock at my front door.

Staring at my mirror image one last time, I give myself a quick pep talk. "Be bold. Be strong. Be adventurous," I say aloud before I turn on my heels and head to the door.

When I pull the door open, Drew's fist is lifted mid-air, and he smiles, but it falters once he gets a full view of me. I'm not sure how to describe the look that crosses his features.

Shock.

Awe.

A mixture of both.

He quickly schools his expression, giving me one of his alluring smirks. I return the gesture with one of my own.

"Rosie." He says my name with a sort of faraway reverence. I understand completely why girls throw themselves at him. He's all charm and confidence. His open demeanor pulls you in with barely a glance, but if he's looking at you, Drew Nallen owns your attention.

Tucking a loose strand of hair behind my ear, I look down at my feet and back up again as his name leaves my lips. "Drew."

"You look amazing," he tells me after another couple of seconds of silence.

My cheeks turn a deep shade of pink. I turn quickly so as not to give away the fact he's just made my night. "Thank you. You look nice, too." I reach for my clutch sitting on the small wooden table next to the door.

When I turn back around, he has that look again on his face I can't quite place, then it quickly disappears. His gaze drifts to mine and for a few seconds, I see that part of him I've caught a glimpse of a few times, but always quickly fades away.

Eyes clear of any emotion, Drew takes my hand and places it through the crook of his arm. "Shall we?" he asks, closing the door behind us.

Looking over at him, I nod, my face glowing with happiness. "We shall," I answer. It's been a while since I've gone on a first date. Four and half years to be exact, but for some reason, I feel at ease. I look over at his face. As usual, he seems calm and collected. "You didn't tell me where we're going."

Glancing at me from the corner of his eye, his lips tilt up on one side.

"No. No, I didn't," he responds, humor in his voice. He sounds playful and happy. This is definitely going to be fun. I think Drew Nallen is the perfect answer to my prayers.

I squeeze his arm and stop thinking about all the what-ifs of this scenario. Instead, I focus on just being with Drew, what I want, and having fun while doing it.

We're sitting at one of my favorite restaurants on the wharf, Reva's. It's been nice so far. Drew has been recounting his day while I've been quietly listening.

It's comfortable being with Drew. I feel extra relaxed, and it has nothing to do with the fact I'm on my second glass of chardonnay. It's just easy to be with him.

Drew clears his throat, pulling me from my thoughts.

"Rosie, I think we need to set some rules. I agreed to do this, and the more I think about it, I'm worried about how you will handle what you're asking of me. I want to be clear about what we're doing," he tells me. I can tell he's honestly concerned.

A burst of laughter slips past my lips, and one of Drew's eyebrows shoots up.

"That's funny, huh?" He smirks.

Nodding my head, I try to say between snorts, "You are so serious."

"This is serious, Rosie. I don't want to hurt you. This isn't something I take lightly. You're my friend. I know who I am and how I live my life. I'm careful when it comes to my personal life." He doesn't look like he finds my laughing cute anymore. Drew is serious.

I quickly wipe the smile from my face.

Reaching my hand across the table, I gently touch his, and he flinches, but I don't pull away. "I'm sorry. I do that when things get too serious or uncomfortable," I try to explain. I wait until he looks up from our hands. "Look, I get who you are. When I told you last night I understand what this whole arrangement will be and what it won't be, I meant it. I'm not one of those girls, Drew, who thinks she can change you. I know what I'm doing. I like you. You're honest. You're kind. I trust you, and that's why I decided you're the one I want to do this with."

Taking a deep breath, I continue while he watches me. "Regardless of your agreement to do this with me, I was going to do it anyway. Hell, I was planning on having this kind of arrangement with a complete stranger. In fact, I was thinking of multiple complete strangers." His mouth falls open, but I go on. "I just got lucky you walked in because I'd be sitting there with either "Boogers McGee" or "Harry and the Hendersons" as my only options at that moment.

This time, he laughs out loud. Isn't it weird how your body can react so strongly to such a simple, normal sound? It isn't only his laugh, though. It's the way his eyes crinkle at the corners like they're laughing right along with him. The best part is I'm the one who made him laugh. I never made Michael laugh.

"You're funny; you know that, Rosie Fisher?" he says between chuckles.

I blush. He makes me do that a lot.

"Seriously, though. You want rules, then let's make rules," I comment. "I'm sure I can come up with some of my own."

"I want to make rules," he states matter-of-factly. "And I wouldn't feel comfortable if you didn't have your own."

I intertwine my fingers, placing my elbows on the table and resting my chin on my hands, and lean forward. "You first," I say.

He mimics my movements. It's like we're having a showdown. Who will crack first?

"Fine. Rule number one, leave all emotional feelings at the door. This is about mutual pleasure, about you getting what you want, and nothing more," he says in a challenging tone. It's like he's trying to scare me away. Well, it won't work. I'm determined to do this, and he's already agreed to it, so I'm not letting him back out now.

"Fine, I say, repeating his sentiment. "I'm changing the agreement a little."

I'm not sure when this idea came to me or why I suddenly want to change the terms of our initial agreement, but I suddenly feel like this is the best way to handle it for both of our sakes. His eyes widen, and he looks like he wants to say something, but he remains silent.

"I don't want to date you casually. I only want to have sex casually with you," I declare.

Drew drops his hands to the table with a thump. "What in the ever loving hell are you talking about, Rosie? Did you just say you only want to have sex with me?"

I can't tell if he is appalled or intrigued. There it is again, the urge to laugh, but I hold it down. I need to be confident because I need him to take me seriously. I mean what I'm proposing to him. I think it may be the only way to guard my heart. Sure, it may not make sense to most people, but if we only have sex for pleasure and no emotions, I can separate myself. Dates will make it harder because the playing field will be bigger and there's more of a chance to feel something I shouldn't. Sex is sex. Or so I'm telling myself.

I push my shoulders back and sit up straight. "That's exactly what I just said. No dates between us. Only sex. I just have one stipulation: I want you to help me change into someone a guy would notice. Someone a guy would want to date. Tell me the rules of how to keep a man's interest. Teach me. Coach me. I want to know how to be a girl someone wants to be with. I also want to be able to have sex and without letting my feelings get involved."

"Let me get this straight. You want me to coach you for dates with other guys, but I get to sleep with you?" He says it like he thinks I'm crazy. Maybe I am.

"It's good to know I made myself clear," I reply with as much sass as I can muster.

"Are you—" he starts to say. I cut him off before he can finish.

"Yes, I'm sure, Drew. I know what I want, and I also know I'm only mentally capable of sleeping with someone I trust. I know. This is a win-win situation for me. And, you still get to have your number one rule. No feelings. No emotions."

I notice a frown before his expression becomes neutral.

"Okay." He sounds resigned to the fact I'm not changing my mind. Good. "How will I coach you if I'm not the one on the date with you?"

"A valid question and I think maybe you should follow me," I suggest then realize that sounds a bit strange. "What I mean is, I'll let you know where I'm going. We'll talk before and after to discuss."

"This is so weird," he interjects. I shrug my shoulders.

"I know, but I need your help," I tell him.

"But, why? You're…" he begins to say.

"I'm boring. I'm plain. I lack experience. Drew, I'm the epitome of safe, and guys don't want mundane. They want more," I proclaim. "I want to be more."

I try to keep the hurt and resentment out of my voice and off my face.

Blinking, he watches me for a moment before speaking. "Alright, I'll go where you go. I'll agree to the arrangement if it's what you really want.

Suddenly, I'm nervous again, so I do what any person with the urge to jump up from her chair and run screaming from the room would do. I pick up my glass of wine and down it. I think Drew knows his consent to my rules has me feeling a little off the solid ground because he's watching me wearing that same crooked grin I've seen time and time again.

We sit silently staring out the window over the silvery ocean until our bill comes. Drew pays it, and we both stand. He quietly takes my hand, leading to the exit. When we walk out into the cool night air, I pull my sweater on to keep from getting a chill.

Drew reaches for my hand again and begins walking forward, but I don't move. Another rule just popped into my head. When I remain standing, Drew turns and looks at me.

"What's wrong?" he asks me, a confused look on his face.

"One more rule," I state plainly.

"Uh…okay," he says, his tone urging me to continue.

"We can go on dates with other people. We can sleep with one another. But, we absolutely cannot sleep with other people. Our sex is monogamous," I instruct, leaving no room for argument.

"You know I don't do serious," he states, the smirk back on his face.

"Well, I don't want an STD or anything. My parents would die if I got the clap or something!" I squeak out, glancing around to see if anyone is near enough to have heard me.

Drew explodes with laughter. He's laughing at me so hard, tears are coming from his eyes. What did I say that was so funny?

Stomping my foot, I shout, "I'm serious!"

He bends over at the waist, hands on his knees, attempting to regain his composure. I stare down at him, watching him laugh, still confused by the fact he is laughing at something so serious.

Drew seems to have finally gotten it together. Straightening, he looks at me, fighting another burst of laughter.

"I'm serious," I whisper this time.

He reaches for my hand, taking it in his, and dips his head to catch my eye. I still see a ghost of a smile on his lips. "I know you are, Rosie, but really? The clap? You couldn't think of any other STD?" A chuckle slips past his lips again.

Shrugging my shoulders, I begin to smile too. "It's the first thing that came to my mind."

He moves his hand to my face, caressing my cheek, and our gazes lock.

"You really are just too adorable for my own good," he tells me sincerely.

There's that damn word again, but for some reason, I don't hate it this time when he says it.

The Decision

Pivotal moment number three happened in my living room...

I decided I knew what I was doing. I decided I was strong.

I didn't know anything.

CHAPTER Six

I'm nervous as hell when Drew walks me to my door. Did we agree to do this tonight? Am I ready?

Oh, shit. I'm not sure anymore. He's standing behind me as I unlock the door. I'm afraid to face him because if I do, what will I see on his face? Will it be desire or just a guy acting like a gentleman by walking his date to the door? I don't know which I prefer.

Once I have the door unlocked, I slowly turn back to face him.

"Thank…you," I stutter out nervously.

He smiles. Just as he did earlier, Drew places his hand on the side of my cheek. "Don't," he whispers. He strokes my cheek softly with his thumb. A shiver runs through my body. It's impossible for my eyes to leave his. "I really like you, Rosie. Are you ready for this?"

Feeling a rush of nerves, I blurt out, "Are we going to have sex now?" I slap my hand over my mouth. God damn it.

Drew raises his eyebrows and his face lights up, but he doesn't laugh at me. I can tell he wants to, but instead he just says, "I thought it might be a good idea."

I can't do anything but nod.

"Are you sure? Because if you aren't, it's okay. I want you to be sure," he continues tenderly.

I feel so safe. It's a feeling I didn't even realize had been missing from my life.

Placing my hand over his, I pull his hand to lead him into my apartment without saying a word. The moment we cross my threshold is the only answer he needs. He whips me around, closing the door at the same time he pushes me up against it.

When our mouths collide with one another, a moan escapes our lips; I'm not sure if it's coming from Drew or me.

It just feels so good. So right. And it's because of that feeling that I suddenly place my hands on Drew's chest pushing him away from me.

"Rosie?" He says my name like a question. Of course he does; one minute I'm just as hot and heavy as he is and then boom, I'm pushing him away.

As I lift my hand to my mouth, tears slowly fall down my face. He takes a step toward me, and I put my hand up between us. He freezes.

"I'm so sorry, Drew. I'm not sure I can do this even if I want it," I confess quietly.

He reaches his hand towards me. "No, Rosie. Don't be sorry. I want you… God, do I want you, but I only want you if you want me too. Come here." He tries to comfort me with his words as he takes my hand, pulling me into his arms.

I go willingly, allowing Drew to draw me into his embrace. *Safe.*

I'm not sure how long we stand there, me in his arms before we move into the living room. He guides me to the couch, pulling me into his lap as he falls onto my overstuffed couch.

"Tell me something, Rosie," he says, pausing until I nod my head against his shoulder. "Who hurt you?"

Safe flutters through my mind again. I feel safe, and because Drew makes me feel this way, I begin to tell him about Michael and what led me to make this agreement with him. He listens without saying a word. He doesn't need to respond to anything I tell him because I can feel every emotion my words bring out in him.

I feel his anger when his heart rate speeds up, and the muscles in his chest tighten. I can feel his protectiveness when his arms gingerly tighten around me. I feel it all, so I keep talking. And he keeps quiet until I come to the part where Michael blamed me for his infidelity and the end of our relationship.

I've moved from his lap; my head now rests on it as he plays with my hair.

"Abbey is the one who encouraged me to put myself out there, but if I'm honest, you're the one who made me actually want something more for myself. Michael was right; I became so boring. So routine. I lost myself in him, and there is no one to blame but myself. I've never been exceptional, but I also never tried to be. I always say the wrong things at the wrong time. I've never been confident or bold or carefree. I could see the moment I looked into your eyes that you are all of those things. You made me want," I reveal to him. I've never quite said those things, my insecurities, to anyone until this moment.

He doesn't stop playing with my hair. "Rosie, don't take the blame for that guy. You aren't to blame because he's an adult and he had a choice. He chose to cheat on you. He chose to give you up. Michael sounds like the biggest dumbass to ever walk the earth because everything I've learned about you over the last couple months tells me you're amazing," Drew tries to assure me.

Sitting up, I face him, placing my arms around his neck. He embraces me tightly.

"Thank you for listening to me. It means so much," I tell him. I glance at the clock, and it's nearly one in the morning. "It's so late; please stay. My couch pulls out into bed. Let me just get you a pillow and blanket."

He hesitates. I can tell he isn't comfortable with the idea of staying. "It won't mean anything. We've had wine, and it's late. Two friends are talking. It will mean nothing," I tell him, unsure if I'm trying to convince him or myself.

He's quiet for a moment longer, searching my face, then says, "Sure, thank you." I stand up without saying a word and make my way over to the linen closet.

When I hand him the blanket and pillow, I rise up on my tiptoes, placing my arms around his shoulders and hugging him lightly.

"Thank you for this…for everything," I breathe.

When I turn away to walk into my bedroom, my heart starts pounding in my chest again, and my mind starts racing. My head hits the pillow, and as much as I wish it, I can't turn off my brain. Drew. Me. Our arrangement. It's clouding every thought even as crawl into bed.

I can't tell you how long I've been lying wide awake, staring up at the ceiling, unable to go to sleep.

It's so quiet, only the sound of my breathing meeting his as it drifts from under the door into my room. The only difference is our rhythm because his is slow and steady and mine is quick and full of trepidation.

My body and mind are in a battle of wills. My heart is unable to pick sides.

I know the rules. I date. He dates. We just don't date one another. Drew and I have sex. We can hold hands, kiss, casual sex, but nothing more. Wanting more is off the table. And we both agreed that can't happen.

I quickly sit up in bed. I can do this, and it doesn't have to mean anything. No expectations. Yes, I'm an adult woman, and I have needs. Only a crazy person would allow someone like Drew Nallen to sleep in the other room on their foldout couch without experiencing everything he is willing and capable of offering. There is no doubt he is capable.

The ache in my body only intensifies at the thought of his competence.

As I push the covers back, my mind is made up; I'm going to take what I need. No strings. Pure satisfaction and nothing more.

Slowly, I tiptoe my way to the door and open it, slipping soundlessly into the living room.

The moonlit room creates the perfect silhouette of Drew lying across the bed. My heart speeds up and for a split second, I consider turning around and letting my fear win. No. He's here, and although I stopped the kiss we shared earlier, I know Drew wanted more at that moment as much as I did.

Lifting the edge of the covers, I gently slip between the sheets. Drew is lying on his back with his head turned away from me. The column of his neck is exposed. I take a tiny breath and guardedly lean forward until my lips press softly against his skin, lingering a moment with each one I place trailing up his neck. I pull back and wait. He doesn't startle awake. Drew blinks, languidly turning his head until his icy blue eyes meet mine. I expected shock or even a reprimand of this reckless decision. Instead, Drew only looks as if he's been expecting me. Waiting for this moment. Waiting for me. I remain propped up on my elbow, staring down at him. His expression remains neutral, but a fire burns between us. We remain still. Staring. Daring one another to move closer to the fire first. Drew moves first, his hand coming up, cradling my face. Our gazes remain locked as he caresses my cheek. Without saying a word, he questions my intentions. I answer by making my way slowly over his body until I'm straddling his hips. He watches me, the flame burning brighter as I lift the hem of my slip over my head, tossing it onto the floor. A smile lights his face when he reaches up and caresses the soft, smooth skin of my stomach before he sits up with me still naked in his lap. "Look me in the eyes, Rosie," he demands in a raspy voice. My eyes don't leave his, and when he knows I'm doing as he asked, Drew continues, "No strings." I ignore the tiny pang I feel in my heart.

"No strings. Just sex," I respond, pure desire in my voice.

The need I'm feeling is all that matters. I want this. Nothing more. As soon as the words leave my mouth, he tangles his hand into my hair, pulling me toward him, molding our mouths together. Our hands explore one another like we've never touched another person before tonight. A moan escapes my lips as Drew pulls away from me and reaches for his discarded jeans on the chair beside us. He quickly pulls something from his pocket. When he looks up at me, he gives me one of his signature crooked smiles and says, "Lesson number two, always protect your heart and always protect your life." Drew holds up his hand and waggles his eyebrows. I let out a quiet giggle. Thank God he's prepared. Suddenly, he's pulling me back against him and flipping me to my back. His hand comes up to my cheek, cupping it gently then moving down my throat. It's as if he's worshipping every part of me and committing it to memory, so he never forgets what this feels like. "You're so beautiful," he whispers. "No matter what you do with all of this, Rosie, please remember who you are is enough." I can't say anything because his hand is moving between us, sending pleasure through me. All I can do is nod in acknowledgment of what he just told me.

He places his large hands around my hips, pushing into me gently. I suck in a breath, closing my eyes, and he pauses until I open them. Slowly, he continues to move his hips forward until he's fully pressed against me. I release a blissful sigh because having him inside me feels so good. Then we're moving together, perfectly in sync. Our hands move over one another, trying to feel everything as our bodies create an explosive friction between us. I've never felt anything like this and breathing is hard, but it doesn't hurt. It doesn't scare me. It only makes me want him more. I want this feeling to last forever, but my body has a different idea. Suddenly, I'm exploding into a million tiny electric pieces. My skin sizzles from head to toe, and my vision blurs. I'm barely able to hear Drew when he moans my name one last time, collapsing against me. Our hearts are pounding against one another in unison, but I'm pretty sure they're beating to a different tune. Mine feeling more and his just feeling satisfied.

We lie side by side, staring up at the high-vaulted ceiling of my living room. I'm trying to wrap my mind around how I feel, wondering what Drew is feeling. My imagination is running wild with his silence. The mood around us is beginning to feel heavy, so I do what I do best. I decide to make awkward conversation.

Looking at him from the corner of my eyes, I watch his face. He has a strange smile set perfectly on his features.

"So, Mr. Nallen, did I make an A?" I ask, propping myself up onto my elbow, facing him.

Turning his head toward me, Drew smirks. "Mr. Nallen?"

Nodding my head, I reply seriously, "Of course, I was taught it isn't respectful to call your teacher by their given name."

Drew erupts into laughter and reaches for me, pulling me on top of his chest. I look down into his bright eyes, shining with humor. "You're adorable," he tells me, and a tiny frown forms on my face. Drew pokes me in the side when he notices, making me giggle. "You, Rosie Fisher, do not need tutoring. I give you an A plus."

I can't control the instant curve of my lips, but then it disappears when doubts set in again.

"Really? Are you sure? Because the last—" I question, but Drew places his finger against my lips to silence me.

"First, stop worrying. Worrying doesn't convey confidence. Second, I'm positive," he tells me, the tone of his voice a little more serious than before.

"I always worry and analyze and then worry some more," I confess quietly.

Drew gets a pensive look on his face like I've just given him a difficult problem to solve. I study his face some more. Now that I'm this close to him, I can see his beauty more clearly. His olive skin is smooth, and his long, full lashes make the perfect frame for his blue eyes. The contrast of his dark skin and hair to his light eyes only adds to the perfection of his Roman nose and strong chin. Drew Nallen is simply one of the most handsome guys I've ever laid eyes on.

He reaches up and pushes the loose hair that has fallen into my eyes, pulling my attention back to our conversation.

"Why do you worry so much? It isn't good for you," he says.

"I've always been a worrier. About everything," I state plainly.

He runs the tip of his finger over my cheekbone, down my small, turned up nose, and back to my cupids bow lips. His touch feels amazing. A shiver runs through me. Something clouds his eyes, but it's gone before I can figure out what it is.

Pulling his hand away, Drew bends both arms and places his hands behind his head on the pillow. The action catches my attention, and I try not to overthink the fact that it appeared deliberate.

After a couple of minutes of silence between us, he quietly sighs.

"You know, you seem to be settling into this whole casual thing. I'm a bit surprised how natural it's coming to you, but you've got to work on the worrying thing. Remember, positive self-talk," he teases, the corner of his mouth tipping up in humor. "Repeat after me: I'm a desirable firecracker in bed." He sounds so serious that I lose it.

A loud, boisterous laugh erupts from me, my body shaking against his chest.

Drew doesn't laugh. "I said, repeat after me, Rosie," he scolds, but he doesn't sound angry.

"I can't," I say between giggles.

He quickly grabs me around the waist and flips me over. Taking my wrist in his skillful hands, Drew pins me against the bed. "Say it. I'm a desirable firecracker in bed."

By this time, I'm laughing so uncontrollably I can barely breathe.

"Say it," he says again.

Laughing, I shout, "I'm a desirable firecracker in bed! Now let me go!"

Drew hovers over me. The biggest grin is covering his face. "I can't! I'm ready for the grand finale."

The Change

Pivotal moment number four, accepting the decision...

CHAPTER Seven

I t was just after four in the morning when we finally fell asleep. I'm not sure how many encores he insisted upon, but as I turn over, I release a long sigh. My eyes still closed, I can feel the sunlight pouring in through the windows, and I wonder what time it is.

Blinking, I try to allow my eyes time to adjust before my gaze drifts to the clock hanging just above the bar in the kitchen.

It's ten thirty in the morning. A slow smile forms on my mouth as I roll toward Drew and reach out for his solid form. I never sleep this late, but I feel so good it is well worth the laziness. The smile and feelings all drain away when my hand falls onto the empty bed sheets.

Pulling the sheet with me, I sit up quickly, glancing around the room for any sign he's still here. I close my eyes and listen for the sound of running water, hanging on tightly to the thought he's in the shower. Nothing. Silence. I can feel the tears beginning to form, but I shut them down quickly. No. I'm not that girl anymore. My mind is made up.

I'm allowing myself one minute, then I'm not thinking about the fact Drew's morning-after disappearance has left me vulnerable, gutted, sick, and cracked. Not broken, but cracked. One minute more…no, forty-five seconds.

In thirty seconds, I'm getting out of this bed. I'm starting my day.

I'm going to drink my coffee. I'm going to go for a run.

In fifteen seconds, I'm going to be me. The me who does laundry on Saturdays. Yep.

In five more seconds, I'm going to be so me. More me than I've ever been. Me, scattered and newly bold me. Uh huh, I'm doing casual like a champ.

With no pity seconds left for me to sulk, I hop out of bed, my hands raised above my head, and yell, "Me!"

It has been decided. I'm totally going to hang out in the casual dating club even if I feel way out of my league.

I ran. I did laundry. Now I'm walking into The Roasting Company to meet up with Abbey.

It has been a perfectly normal Saturday with the exception I was left alone in bed after a night of sex with Drew, I still haven't heard from him, and I've ignored the sick feeling in the pit of my stomach all day.

Yep, perfectly normal.

As I wait in line, Andy peeks his head over the crowd and calls out to me in a greeting. "Good Morning, Rosie!"

"Good morning, Andy," I reply more cheerfully than I feel. Seeing Andy does make me feel somewhat better. It usually does. His aura exudes positivity. I'm going to latch on to it this morning and accept that I made choices. I'm going to revel happily in the choice I made and the fact that I had the best sex of my life multiple times last night.

Smiling, I finally make it to the counter to order.

"The usual?" Andy asks as he waves at someone who just entered the shop. He makes eye contact, a question forming in his expression. I recognize the moment he decides to let it go.

"Yes, please," I confirm then continue, "and Abbey is meeting me, so add a large hazelnut mocha with an extra shot."

"You got it." He grins at me. "As usual, it's lovely to see you,

Rose, my dear."

I smile, and he winks.

When I turn around, I scan the room for him. Why? I'm not quite sure. I don't recall him ever mentioning he comes in here on Saturdays. As my eyes roam over the faces sitting around the room, a table of familiar faces catches my attention.

They all wave me over, so I make my way across the room.

It's a daily routine for me to spend at least twenty minutes sitting with this little group of four…five…six… It changes daily. Most days it's just the four of them: Lenny, Marti, Lorna, and Colleen. Andy introduced us when I first moved to Santa Cruz and began coming into the coffee shop regularly. They're all retired and meet every morning to chat over coffee. They all welcomed me into their little club with open arms. I can't imagine my life without them.

I can't imagine this shop without them. Just like Lynn, they greet me daily with a warm smile and a wave.

As I approach the table, Marti stands up and pulls me into a tight hug.

"Hey, honey, what's happening?" she asks as she pulls away, kissing me on the cheek in the process. Colleen is sitting behind her, waving at me with a big grin on her face.

"Hey, not much. Just meeting my friend, Abbey."

I take a seat between Marti and Colleen. Lenny is in the middle of a debate with Lorna. A typical occurrence.

"Rosie, nice to see you, honey," Lenny says in between trying to convince Lorna that Bernie Sanders is our nation's best option. It brings a smile to my face as I watch this seventy-something-year-old man wearing his "Feel the Bern" t-shirt. I'm not even sure Lorna disagrees with him, but our nation's political turmoil has been the hot topic for months now.

"Hey, Lenny," I return his greeting, but he's already back to having his conversation with Lorna.

Lorna looks over at me, although Lenny is in the middle of a monologue, and says, "Drew just walked in." She states it so matter-of-factly my mouth falls open. I freeze. It's amazing to me; she hardly says anything, yet I'm positive she sees all. Why she thinks I would have any care for the fact Drew just walked in is beyond me. When I look at her because I can't do anything else, she gives me a crooked grin and turns her attention back to Lenny, who hasn't stopped talking, except now he has pulled Colleen and Marti into the conversation.

I glance over my shoulder. Drew's back is to me. I quickly stand, wave goodbye, and sit in at a corner table to wait for Abbey. Looking down at my watch, I grimace. Where is she?

I hear Andy greet Drew. This is bad. I'm totally not avoiding him. I asked for this, and I got what I wanted. We're friends, and how in the hell is he going to help me if I'm avoiding him? I'm acting ridiculous. I'm being the old Rosie.

Just as the thought crosses my mind, I feel a warm pair of lips on my cheek. This is definitely isn't Abbey. Suddenly, Drew is sitting across from me, giving me that damn signature Drew Nallen smirk. I want to scream at him. Demand he explain his disappearance and the fact he hasn't called or sent a simple text of thanks for all the sex. Instead, I can't resist showing my pleasure at seeing him.

"Rosie Fisher, you're a hard lady to track down," he announces, a teasing tone to his voice.

I'm confused. "I am?" I question.

Nodding, he takes a sip of his coffee. He looks so good, and the way his tongue darts out to wet his lip brings up visions of last night. "Yep, I would've called, but I left my phone at your apartment. I've stopped by there twice already today, and you haven't been home. I figured I'd try here, and if it were a dead end, I would still win because I can always use a cup of coffee."

"Oh. You left your phone. Thank God," I say. Out loud. Damn it. Drew gives me a questioning look. Trying to change the direction of his thoughts quickly, I continue, "I'm supposed to meet Abbey, but if you give me an hour or so, I can meet you at my apartment so you can get it."

He stares at me for a moment before he speaks. "Rosie, were you upset because you think I didn't call you?"

"No!" I exclaim a little too loudly. Damn it. I said I could handle this and I can. "Look, Drew, I had a momentary lapse of monogamous desires. I'm new to this whole casual thing, so I may have gotten a little butt hurt over it. For like a minute. Literally. One minute," I tell him, almost apologetically.

"Butt hurt?" He looks as if he wants to laugh. At me. Again.

"Yep, it means my feelings were a little hurt when they really shouldn't be. Ya know, butt hurt?" I explain.

Shaking his head, he responds, quietly laughing at the same time. "Nope. I don't know."

"Oh damn it, it's just one of many sayings my mama said my whole life. Sorry, I can't help it. It's like Southern diarrhea of the mouth. I can't stop it no matter how much I try," I apologize. When I look at his face, I realize I should've just stopped talking. Did I actually just say diarrhea of the mouth to Drew? He's still looking at me, so I start talking again. "I'm fine now. No biggie. Feelings all good. I'm totally fine and decided I'm totally happy about all the sex we had last night."

There's that damn lip quirk again.

Drew slides his hand across the table and takes mine. "I'm totally happy about it, too. Also, I would've called, but my phone. As for the Southern diarrhea of the mouth, I like it. It's cute, even if the sayings are a little weird."

I can't help but laugh. I really like Drew Nallen.

"Are you still sure about our little arrangement?" he mentions, bringing his coffee to his mouth again for another drink. How is that so attractive?

Drew is watching me, probably analyzing my every move and expression. His forehead is slightly creased like he's worried about something.

"Yes, I'm still fine." I try to keep my voice neutral.

He squeezes my hand lightly. "You can be honest with me, Rosie. We're friends. I care about you."

Placing my other hand over his, I imitate him by squeezing his hand.

"Really, Drew, I'm fine. There was a minute I felt a little sad you weren't there when I woke up, but I realized that's part of it. That is our arrangement. That is a casual sex kind of thing. And that is what we have. Staying the whole night is a completely different relationship," I assure him.

"I worried about that, and I left because I never stay. I never stay, Rosie. It isn't you. It's every time I sleep with someone. I always go home, okay?" He sounds as if he is begging me for forgiveness when honestly, I know the situation, and there's nothing to forgive.

"Drew, stop. We're good," I reassure him again.

"We're good." His voice sounds a little distant. I don't like it.

"Okay, you're still game to help me, right? Because Abbey is supposed to help set me up for some online dating." I take our conversation into another direction in hopes he doesn't get the wrong idea and think I can't handle this little deal we made.

Drew has a strange look on his face, one I've seen a few times over the last couple of days, but then it quickly transforms into something else more recognizable. The look of the cool, calm, and collected Drew I'm used to seeing.

"Online dating? Huh? Are you sure about that?" He doesn't sound like he thinks online dating is the best idea.

"Yep, is that bad? I don't know how this works," I respond, feeling even more worried about the idea than I was before his remark.

"I guess not," he says, still sounding unsure. We stare at one another, a strange vibe between us. Then he stands up. "Well, I'm going to get going. Let me know when our first coaching session will be."

He leans down, placing another soft kiss to my cheek. I smile, but it's a little forced. I can't help feeling a little uneasy about the way Drew is acting.

"I will," I tell him, still watching him closely.

He gives me that smirk again, but this time, it's a little off. When he turns to leave, I realize we didn't make a plan for him to get his phone back.

Abruptly standing, I grab his arm before he can leave. "We didn't decide what time you'll come by to get your phone."

"No, we didn't. When will you be home? I only have one more errand to run today," he tells me, still not really looking me in the eyes.

"I should be home in an hour," I tell him. I'm still holding on to his arm, and he still isn't looking at me.

"I'll see you then," he responds, but he doesn't move. He waits for me to let his arm go. I hesitate then slowly let him go.

"Yeah, okay I'll see you," I reiterate.

I'm left watching a retreating Drew and wondering what exactly went wrong. Did we make a mistake? I may be unsure about most things in my life, but I know for sure I always want Drew in it.

CHAPTER
Eight

Two hours later, I'm at home putting away the last bit of laundry I was too lazy to put away earlier, and still no Drew.

Maybe he decided he didn't need his phone after all. That doesn't really make sense, though. Of course, he would need his phone. If I really think about it, we didn't set an exact time. I only said I'd be home in an hour, and he said he would see me.

As I'm closing the drawer on my dresser, the doorbell rings, startling me from my thoughts.

It must be Drew, and my body must know it too because I'm suddenly nervous. I can't pinpoint exactly why, but I think it has everything to do with the way he was acting when he left me at the coffee shop earlier.

I take a deep breath then turn the locks on the door before opening it.

He's standing there looking perfectly and beautifully normal. There is something different about his expression than it looked when he walked away. Drew is giving me his usual naturally smoldering look. A look I'm certain he doesn't even realize he makes; he's just being Drew.

"Hey, sorry I'm later than I said I would be. I had to drop something off at my parents' house. Of course, I got stuck there talking to my mom. It had been a while since I was there last, so I felt bad running in and out," he apologizes.

"Hey, don't worry about it. I wasn't going anywhere, and we didn't set an exact time," I assure him. Opening the door wider, I invite him in. "Come in. I'll get your phone."

Heading for the table, I walk over to retrieve his phone. I can hear the door close behind me. I pick up his phone and turn back to face Drew. He's standing in front of the bookshelf in my living room, looking at the framed photos of my family and me. He picks up a photo taken just last summer when they came here to visit. Drew lets out a small laugh. He doesn't even have to tell me what he's laughing at because I laugh every time I look at the photo, too. The sound of his laugh and the thought of the picture brings a warm, burning feeling of happiness into my chest.

The photo is of me, my parents, and my siblings. Michael is in it too. We're all standing near the Lighthouse on West Cliff. The breeze was blowing lightly around us. My mom was complaining about the chill in the air, yet it was seventy-two degrees. Michael and I are the only ones wearing short sleeves and shorts while my family practically looked like they were visiting the Arctic. Every time they have visited me over the last three years, my family just can't seem to get used to the climate change from Texas.

Drew faces me, lifting the picture in the air, another laugh slipping out before he sets it down on the shelf again.

I shrug my shoulders and let a giggle slip out, too. "My family just can't seem to get used to our warm California summers," I joke. "They were freezing that day."

His lips tip up, a soft, happy look on his face as he contemplates my words.

"You seem to do just fine in our weather here. Do you miss the really hot summers?" Drew comments, making his way over to me and taking his phone when I extend it toward him.

I look at him, appalled by the statement. "You're kidding, right?" I ask.

"No, I've always wondered what it's like to live in a place with all of the seasons," Drew replies as he walks over and takes a seat on the couch, slipping his flip-flops off before putting his feet up on the coffee table.

"No, not at all. It gets plenty warm enough here for me. Plus, the beauty that surrounds us here far outweighs the need for almost constant heat. Forget about the cold weather in Texas. I definitely never miss that," I add as I take a seat next to him, pulling my bare feet up onto the couch with me. I sigh wistfully. "But the spring and fall, I do miss."

"I've traveled a lot, but I've never lived anywhere but Santa Cruz. I don't think I could," he reveals. It seems so personal for some reason, although it's so simple.

"I love being from Texas. I love Texas. I always will, but Santa Cruz has been home since the moment I drove into town. I felt it to my core. I miss my family, but living away from here is like missing a part of myself," I admit to him. Sometimes I feel like it's a betrayal to my family, but it's the truth. I was meant to live here; I just haven't figured out exactly why yet.

When I look over at Drew, he's watching me intently. It's not the first time over the last few days I've noticed this look on his face. I'm sure he thinks I'm the strangest individual he knows. I know Michael thought so; he told me many times that my brain just didn't quite function like the rest of the world. He called it my bubble. Drew must be trying to figure out how my bubble works in the real world.

The look on his face suddenly changes into something different, and he says, "I don't think people are always born where they're supposed to be. Some have to go out and look for their place in life. This must be your place."

That simple statement from him brings on an unexpected joyful feeling for me. "Thank you for saying that," I tell him sincerely.

His happiness mirrors the joy on mine.

Without thinking, I crawl to his end of the couch and climb onto his lap. He stiffens at first, but as I look down into his eyes, he relaxes. I just stare at him, and he stares back, unmoving except for the beat of our hearts beneath our chests. Ever so slowly, I lean into him until our lips touch. I run my tongue over his lips. Drew still hasn't moved, but his eyes are closed now. Normally, I would feel shy. I would think I'm doing something wrong because it seems like he isn't responding to my touch. I'd be wrong because right now I'm reading his body language and all the signs are there. His heartbeat is strong and fast. I feel the way I'm making Drew feel, and he literally hasn't moved. His heartbeat is telling me. The way his breathing has changed lets me know he is affected by my touch and his eyes are closed like he's savoring the moment. I feel confident, which is a surprise to me because I've never felt this way in such an intimate position in my life. This excites me, which only makes me want more. More of this feeling. More of Drew. I put my hands on either side of his face, pulling him closer and kissing him deeper. I coax his lips apart until I can explore every inch of his mouth. As soon as our tongues meet, Drew moves for the first time. He wraps his arms around me and attempts to pull me even closer. Soon, he's lifting me up in his arms and standing. He deepens our kiss as he continues to invade me with his mouth as he makes his way to my room. When he reaches my bed, he lays me down gently, never breaking our kiss. As he hovers over me, we stare unmoving into each other's eyes. Then, as if he can't hold back any longer, Drew begins kissing down my neck to the top of my breast. His hands are tugging at the loose pair of cotton shorts I'm wearing, pulling them off along with my panties, tossing them to the floor. He kisses his way back up to my lips, kissing me softly before pulling back and looking into my eyes again. "You still want this? You want what I can offer?" he asks me. I can see the fear on his face at the thought I may say no. He doesn't realize I have the same fear. "Yes, I know the stakes, Drew," I answer, my voice full of unfulfilled desire. He straightens up, pulling his shirt over his head. I pull my tank top off at the same time and throw it off the side of the bed. Our eyes never leave each other. I sit up, unbuttoning his jeans and pulling everything over his hips, letting them drop to the floor. I suck in a deep breath at the sight of him. I doubt I'd ever get tired of looking at him. All of a sudden his mouth is back on mine, sucking and urging me to open up for him. Kissing Drew feels amazing. I feel worshiped. He pulls away for a moment, and I moan at his sudden absence. I realize he's only left me to protect us. There it is again, that feeling of safety. Before I know it, he's back. Hovering over me, Drew moves his hand down my body, feeling his way as if he's trying to mark me as his own. Which is a ridiculous thought? I'll never be only his, nor he only mine. The thought is fleeting because he keeps exploring me. When he reaches down between us, I arch my back involuntarily, filled with the need for more. "Please, Drew..." I beg. It's like he was waiting for me to ask, because as soon as his name leaves my mouth, he buries himself inside of me. My name is like a cry from his lips. "Rosie." He freezes only a moment, but it feels like longer and I need him to move. I need him closer even though it isn't possible. "My God, Rosie. It's like...it's like you..." he whispers, but he never finishes what he started to say; he only moves faster, our bodies moving together in unison. He thrusts into me deeper, harder, a quiet whimper leaving my lips with every move. I lift my hips slightly, trying the impossible task of getting closer to him, but the effect is still rewarding as it creates an altogether alluring sensation between our bodies. Our kisses become hungrier, our tempo becoming a frenzy of movements as our moans become more intense. We don't slow down until we both cry out the other's name. I keep feeling more, but it isn't the more I was looking for when I made this deal with Drew. I'll think about that later though because right now, I'm going to savor in the fact Drew just rolled to his side, pulling me closer and curving his body around me. Neither of us says a word, and soon we both fall asleep feeling good and satisfied. My body, my mind, and my soul feel connected to something good. I just feel so happy. Until I wake up an hour later all alone.

CHAPTER Nine

It's been a little over a week since the new and improved Rosie Fisher made her entrance into the world and got all adventurous. Over the last week, I've adjusted to the idea of having sex and only sex with Drew. We meet for coffee before work, chat, and everything appears normal.

When I first brought up the fact Abbey came over after work on Monday night and set me up for online dating, Drew seemed to change the subject. When I told him on Wednesday I have my first date set for a few days later, he only said, "So soon?" I just don't get him. He must really have something against online dating.

Later that day, when Drew called, it was only to ask me what time my date was and where he needed to meet me. The conversation was short because he immediately said he had to go.

He hasn't been to my house since last Saturday, so we've had little to no physical contact. It's felt a little strange, but I guess that's the way this whole casual friends-with-benefits thing works.

There's a knock on my door, interrupting my thoughts.

When I open the door, Abbey is standing there with her fashion bag, as she calls it, and a few outfits. I told her I had something already picked out, but she said she didn't trust me.

"Hey, have you showered yet?" she asks me as she whisks past me into the apartment.

"I'm not sure why it matters, but yes," I respond, shaking my head as I watch her walk into my room and throw everything on my bed, and then over to the kitchen where she begins pouring two glasses of wine.

"It matters because we need time to get you ready," she chides. "Did you shave your legs?" Abbey takes a big gulp from her wine, handing me a glass as she passes me, walking back into my room.

"Of course, but again, why does it matter if I shaved or not?" She is so annoying sometimes, but damn if I'm not reminded why I love her when she turns around holding up a deep red dress she brought for me to try on.

"It will matter when this guy is rubbing his hand up your legs and into your panties," Abbey states as if I'm a ridiculous person for even asking such a questions.

"Yeah, that won't be happening," I inform her, walking over and taking the red dress from her.

Standing in front of the full-length mirror, I hold the dress up to me.

Abbey is suddenly standing behind me, looking over my shoulder, a confused, slightly exasperated look on her face. "Why the hell not? This is what we talked about!"

"It won't be happening because that's not part of the plan. I'm only going on dates; Drew will coach me along, but the only person I will be sexing it up with is Drew," I advise her, feeling so sure about this arrangement.

"You said you slept with Drew, but you never said you were sleeping with Drew. What in the hell is going on?" she demands. I look at Abbey's reflection in the mirror, and she literally looks appalled by the suggestion I would be only with Drew.

"What's going on is this…I'm going to be going on dates until I find someone I like—*if* I find someone I like. You told me to have casual sex, so I'm doing it. I'm just only doing it with Drew because Drew doesn't date. He doesn't commit. So to avoid attachment, we're only sleeping together. And only with each other. We can date who we want without the intimacy," I explain.

"So what happens if you find someone you like, someone you want to sleep with? What happens then?" she asks with a hint of sarcasm.

"I tell Drew. We stop sleeping together. We go back to being just friends, and we go on about our business. Me with the new guy and Drew with a different girl practically every night like he normally does," I say, doing a fantastic job of sounding nonchalant even though my stomach turns at the thought.

"Oh, wow! Silly me. It looks like you have this all worked out perfectly," Abbey responds.

If I wanted to analyze her response, I might say she spoke with a lot of cynicism.

My number one rule with this online dating is I'll always meet the guy at our chosen destination. He will never pick me up at my house. It also gives me an opportunity to meet with Drew for a little instruction.

We decided this was the best for our arrangement. I'd print out the details of the guy, give them to Drew, and he'd help me go over some ideas of how I should act, so it's not a total disaster. Drew also likes the thought he can keep an eye on me during the dates in case they turn out to be whack jobs. I think he's a bit overprotective.

When I walk into the restaurant around six o'clock, I immediately spot Drew. He's sitting at the bar, sipping on a drink while he chats with the bartender. I'm always struck by how handsome he is, and it sends a tingle up my spine.

Shaking the thought away, I make my way toward Drew.

We only have thirty minutes before my date, a guy named Dan, will be here. I pull out the empty stool next to Drew, smiling brightly at him when he looks over at me. He does a double take; as usual, my skin turns the color of a strawberry at his response.

He quickly stands, placing his hand on my lower back and leaning in close to my ear, his breath against my skin. "You're gorgeous," he whispers. He places a kiss on my neck that makes me want to melt into the floor.

But, instead, I glare at him.

"What was that? You can't do that when I'm on a date with someone else," I scold him, attempting to sound madder than I actually feel.

He takes a step closer to me, peering down into my eyes because although I'm wearing heels, Drew still towers over me. A lump forms in my throat, and I can't speak. "You're not on your date yet," he tries to reason.

"Oh," is all I can manage to say because the way he's looking at me is paralyzing.

"Do you want a drink?" Drew asks me, changing the subject and the mood around us.

"No, I…I…think I'll wait," I stammer out.

Drew indicates for me to sit, so I do. The bartender comes by and looks at me. "Can I just get some water?" I ask him, still feeling a little uneasy. He nods, grabs a glass, fills it, then sets it in front of me before turning to another customer.

Drew has taken his seat next to me once again.

"Okay, let me see it," he tells me, reaching his hand out to me.

Opening my purse, I pull out the profile sheet I printed early in the day. I hand it to Drew, and he begins reading the details out loud.

"Dan Piper. Age 32. Never married. Enjoys surfing and hiking." Drew rolls his eyes when he reads the hobbies. I elbow him in the side, and he just looks at me. "He sounds…great…perfect," he announces once he's done reading the entire profile. "Handsome, too. I guess." I ignore his tone.

"So now what?" I ask him because I have no idea what exactly happens in this part of the plan.

"Well, I've been trying to figure why you need me all day long. I haven't figured it out yet; you're great without my help," he compliments me in his Drew way.

"But I do. I have no idea how to act on a date because other than dinner the other night with you, I haven't been on a date with anyone other than Michael. And we both know how that ended. Oh, God, I'm probably going to bore this Dan guy to death. What in the heck am I going to talk about with him? I'm a copy editor for crying out loud. The most exciting and intrepid thing I've done is have sex with you without a commitment! Twice!" By the time I stop talking, I'm shouting and panicking.

Drew starts rubbing circles with his hand slowly on my back. "Calm down; it's going to be fine. Don't panic. Take a deep breath and maybe talk a little lower next time." There's laughter in his voice. The sound helps me relax, and a giggle slips past my lips.

"Did I just yell to a restaurant full of people that we've had sex?" I laugh, and an unladylike snort escapes me, which only causes me to laugh harder.

Drew's looking at me with that strange look again, and then he's laughing, too.

I'm not sure how long we laugh, but when it subsides, he takes my hand into his and laces our fingers together. He isn't smiling anymore. Neither am I. I have that strange feeling I usually feel when I'm with Drew.

"I figured it out," he says quietly.

Looking away from our hands, I turn toward his face. "What?"

"I figured out why you need me...here." He is sitting next to me; we're mere inches apart, but his voice sounds so far away.

"Oh." Once again, it's the only thing I can think to say in response.

He lifts his gaze from our interlaced hands up to my face. "You need me to remind you." He pauses to take a breath as if he's been holding it instead of talking. When he speaks again, his eyes are clear. "I'm here to remind you how incredibly funny you are and that you have so much to say and offer someone. I'm here to calm you." He raises our hands to his lips and places a soft kiss to mine. "If this guy is worthy, he'll see how great you are. Just believe in yourself."

They're probably the sweetest and most kind words anyone has ever spoken to me. He's right. I need him to keep me calm.

"Thank you," I tell him so quietly, I don't think he hears me at first.

Then he whispers back, "You're welcome."

This whole night has been strange, and my date is even more strange. Don't get me wrong; he's nice enough, everything he said he was on his profile. Dan is actually more handsome in person than in his profile photo. From that perspective, it appears I've picked a keeper, except that isn't the only perspective.

He literally questions everything I put in my mouth.

When we're seated at our table, I order a glass of chardonnay. As soon as the waiter brings it to our table and I take my first sip, Dan asks me if I have any idea what the grapes were fermented in. *What? Excuse me?* I want to say from the taste of it, it was fermented in deliciousness. Instead, I answer honestly that no, I don't have a clue. He proceeds to tell me I may be poisoning myself with sulfites. I haven't taken another drink.

When we order our food, he politely interrogates the waiter about the cooking process for what seems like the entire menu. He glances at me and informs me that the chicken piccata is safe to eat because the chicken used had free range, and all the other ingredients are truly organic. I lose my appetite after he describes the way non-free range chickens are handled and processed.

Now I'm sitting here, stomach growling, wishing I were drunk so I wouldn't think about how hungry I am, and listening to my date regale a story about his West Indies tour last summer. He sounds fun— *sounds* being the key word in this equation.

My mind begins to drift, and I suddenly remember I haven't noticed Drew in a while. Earlier he was seated at a table across the restaurant. I caught him watching us several times, and I tried to make him stop by giving him my evil eye. He only laughed at me and raised his drink in the air as if toasting me.

My eyes begin to search the room until they finally land on him sitting at the bar again.

He's looking directly at me and our eyes meet. When he knows he has my attention, he gives me his signature grin. I smile back, tucking a loose hair behind my ear. I watch him pick up his phone and begin typing. When he finishes, he looks back up and points at me then at his phone.

Dan is still talking, something about a bus and chickens, completely oblivious to my lack of interest.

I slip my hand into my purse, pulling my phone out and setting it in my lap under the table. I tap the screen, and it lights up. There's a text from Drew, and I smile at what I read.

Drew: *Make an excuse. Say you have an emergency and meet me at your apartment.*

I can't do that. It would be rude. I lift my gaze back to him and shake my head. Just about the same time, Dan asks me if I want dessert, so he thinks I'm answering him. Damn it; I want dessert.

"It's probably a good idea; the cream used in the Crème Brulee is probably full of hormones," he decides. "Please excuse me for a moment while we wait for the waiter to bring our check." As he gets up, he looks down at me and smiles. This smile tells me he thinks this is going really well. It makes me a little sad for him, but then I kind of feel pissed off he is oblivious to the fact I haven't eaten a thing the entire meal.

My phone lights up again, so I look down and read the incoming text from Drew.

Drew: *Seriously, Rosie. Hurry up. This guy isn't the guy for you, and I'm tired of waiting.*
Rosie: *How can you tell he isn't the one from across the room?*

His reply is almost immediate.

Drew: *Because I've watched your face all night. You haven't touched your food, and you barely took a sip of your wine. I know you.*

He's not worthy. Now get your pretty little ass to your apartment. I'll be there waiting.

It amazes me Drew has been at least fifty feet across the room from us all night, and he noticed everything and read my mood, but my date is a mere foot away and didn't notice a thing. Damn it. I need an excuse.

CHAPTER Ten

When I walk off the elevator of my fifth-floor apartment, I'm immediately off my feet and hanging over a muscled shoulder, which I can only assume belongs to Drew. I let out a squeal, laughing as he slaps me on the ass. "You scared the be-jeezus out of me!" I laugh, barely able to get the words out.

"Well, that's what you get for making me wait!"

"Just put me down!" I exclaim.

"No," he answers as he rounds the corner of the hallway. When we are almost to the door of my apartment, Drew turns so I can unlock the door. Once I have it unlocked, I twist the knob and push the door open, still hanging upside down.

"Welcome to my humble abode," I tease. He slaps my ass again. He turns back around, walking through the door and closing it behind us. He drops his keys to the floor, so I follow suit, dropping my purse and keys. They land with a clank. Drew doesn't stop walking until he enters my room. He allows me to slide down the front of his body; my arms wrap around his neck. Once we are eye to eye, our lips are mere inches apart; I feel the powerful tension in the air. We don't move, though; we let it build while our breath mingles between us. Then slowly he leans in, his mouth tenderly touching mine. When he pulls back, I can only imagine my eyes look as dazed as his do. "I've wanted to do that since the moment you walked up next to me in the bar at the restaurant tonight." There's a reverence to his voice. "Me too," I confess, crushing my lips against his. Wrapping my legs around his waist, he walks me over to the bed, kissing me feverishly the entire time. He groans when he sets me down as if it hurts to break contact. He reaches behind me, slowly unzipping my dress, letting it fall to the floor and pool at my feet. As he looks at me, he sucks in a breath. We both finish undressing quickly, and Drew rolls a condom on and pulls me onto the bed with him.

Unable to wait another second, we pull one another closer, his hungry mouth devouring mine. Pushing him onto his back, I crawl up his body, my legs resting on either side of his hips as I lower myself, feeling every inch of him connect with my body. The sensation of being with him vibrates through my whole body. For once, I take complete control, moving faster as he moans my name over and over. The sound only increasing the pleasure I feel with him inside of me. We both savor every touch. I push us both until we completely unravel into one another, utterly spent. Exhausted, I lie across his chest, listening to his heartbeat. It thumps to a beat I'm becoming more and more familiar with. And that scares me more than not being enough for someone.

Andy makes his way around the counter when I enter The Roasting Company. He already has my drink of choice in his hand. He hugs me after he hands me the cup of coffee.

"I've missed you," he tells me. It always feels good to be near Andy. There is just something about him.

"I've missed you, too," I reply. We pull apart, smiles on our faces.

"How are things?" he asks as he walks with me to one of the small tables at the center of the coffee shop and we take a seat.

I take a careful drink before answering him. "Honestly, things have been going really well. Work's good. Life's great. I feel good. I even made it to a yoga class this past week. What about you?"

"Things have been good. You know me, I'm enjoying my moments in time," he tells me, an answer he gives me every time we talk. I like hearing it. The sentiment is one I find comforting.

We both stand at the same time; his break is over, and I need to get to work.

I lean in and give him another hug. We say our goodbyes and see you laters. As I'm walking out the door, I wonder for a moment if that is what Drew and I are having together. Just moments in time.

I want to ask Andy how he does it. How he can simply find someone who makes sense, who makes him feel good and happy, but be satisfied and happy with the time he's allowed with them.

Moments in time, I think again. I like Drew and my moments. I feel good and happy, but can the knowledge that this time with him is nothing more than that be enough?

I'm reading the front page of the Good Times newspaper as I leave the coffee shop. It's the reason I don't notice Drew crossing the street toward me.

"Hey, gorgeous!" he hollers at me just before he reaches the curb.

I last saw Drew right before I fell asleep last night. As usual, I woke up alone. I realized after our second night together I was never going to get used to it.

Looking up from the paper, I can't keep from lighting up at the sight of his approaching figure.

"Hey, are you meeting me tomorrow night?" I ask him.

"Meeting you?" He looks confused by my question.

"Didn't you get my text I sent you this morning? I have another date," I inform him.

He looks at me like I just punched him in the gut, but quickly changes his expression. He places the crooked smile on his face. The one I don't like. The one that tries to impersonate the real one, but fails every time.

"Uh, yeah. Sure. Of course, I'll be there," he tells me.

Something is off, but I can't quite put my finger on it.

"You okay?" I ask, concerned.

"Me? Yes, I just haven't had my morning coffee yet, and boy do I need it. Someone kept me up all night," he teases. Something is still off with him, though. "I'll talk with you later."

Drew turns and walks away quickly, leaving me staring at his retreating figure.

I hurry after him. "Drew, wait!" I call after him.

He stops, turning to face me. There it is again. He's forcing a smile.

"What's going on?" I question him pleadingly.

"What do you mean?" he responds, placing his hands on his hips.

"You're acting weird, and I just wanted to be sure you're okay," I tell him.

He watches me. His eyes are searching my face like he's having an inner debate and struggling with the right words. I remain silent. My mom has always told me that if you remain silent, people eventually tell you things. She says when you interrupt them, they almost always leave the important stuff out.

"Rosie, I'm good. I just really want a cup of coffee, and I need to get to work," Drew finally answers.

I study his face. It's the truth, but it isn't the whole truth. Before I can respond, his phone rings and he answers it. "Hey." There's a sweetness to his voice and his eyes avoid me as he listens. "Yeah, of course. We're still on for tonight. I'll pick you up around seven. Great, bye."

The conversation was brief, but as short as it was, I felt what seemed like a lifetime worth of pain. He's going on a date. I knew he would be. It's part of the deal. I'm going on dates, so why would he stop? When I look up, he's watching me, so I blurt out the first thing that comes to my mind. "A date? You're…ah…you have a date. Awesome. Anyone I know?"

He seems confused by my comment and says, "Uh, no. I doubt it."

"Okay, well are you sure nothing else is bothering you?" I ask, changing the subject back to our original topic.

"Rosie, I'm fine, but I really do need to get going," he tells me.

Leaning forward, he places a light kiss on my cheek. It tingles under the skin where his lips touch.

"Okay," I say, realizing I shouldn't push this anymore. If he wanted to tell me what was bothering him, he would.

"See you tomorrow night," he says in parting, then he turns away from me again.

I'm not sure how long I stand there staring in the direction he retreated, but I'm five minutes late for work today.

CHAPTER *Eleven*

A s I enter the office, Abbey is waiting for me by my desk. She smiles when she sees me, and I can tell she's up to something. "There's someone I want you to meet!" she says excitedly.

I walk around her, setting my purse and coffee on my desk before acknowledging her.

Hand on my hip, I roll my eyes at her. "Who is it? I'm not sure I trust you; we've been through this before if you remember correctly," I remind her.

"This is different, I promise. Travis is funny, and he has a great job!" she insists.

Abbey really does look excited about this guy.

"A great job?" I remark sarcastically.

"Yes, and he's kind. He comes from a great family. He isn't afraid to laugh and has been known to stick his awkward foot in his mouth. He's you!" she rattles off. She's practically shouting, and Bernadette leans out of her office, shushing us.

Abbey turns and flips her the bird once Bernadette is back in her office. I just laugh. Abbey has no thought over the fact that she just flipped our supervisor off.

Even though she acts like she doesn't care, Abbey lowers her voice. "Seriously, Rosie. He's hot, and there is no doubt in my mind that he's good in bed!"

I was almost convinced until she said that. Abbey hasn't stopped pushing me to sleep with my dates even after I explained my agreement with Drew. It's like she isn't hearing what I'm saying to her.

"Abbey, I told you this already, I'm only dating. No sex," I say in a low voice so no one else will hear me.

"That's a lie. You're having sex," she retorts.

Well, she has me there. I am having sex. Lots of sex. Lots of good sex. Wait, that's wrong. I'm having lots of great sex. A smile creeps on my face.

"Dude, see, you're thinking about having sex!" she exclaims.

I roll my eyes. "Fine. I'm having sex. I'm just not having sex with anyone I'm going on dates with," I admit.

Shaking her head, Abbey sits on the corner of my desk. "Damn it, Rosie. What are you doing?"

"Well, I'm supposed to be working, but instead, I'm standing here listening to you yap," I tell her, although I know this isn't what she meant.

She stands up, a scowl on her face. "Don't be an asshole! You know I was not referring to your actions at this very moment. What are you doing with Drew? With your life?" Her face is a little red. I think she's actually mad at me, which is weird because I'm not sure if she's ever been mad at me before.

"I'm doing what you told me to do! I'm dating! I'm having casual sex!" This time, I'm the one shouting. Realizing this, I lower my voice. "I'm doing everything we talked about, but I'm choosing only to have meaningless yet pleasurable safe sex with Drew."

This time, Abbey rolls her eyes then looks back at me seriously. "That's just it, I don't believe it's meaningless," she snaps. "Can you honestly say this arrangement you have with Drew means nothing?"

I stare at her, unable to speak.

"If you can admit that to me, then I will never say another word about it. But I don't think you can say that because it means a lot more than you're willing to acknowledge," she says with regret in her voice.

I fall back into my desk chair, staring at my hands until I finally find the words.

"It doesn't matter. I know what is between Drew and me. We have trust and friendship. So you're right, it isn't meaningless. It's just safe. The most important thing is I know what it's not," I divulge.

Abbey is looking at me in a way I don't even want to think about.

"Okay," is all she whispers before turning away and heading toward her desk.

I call after her, "Abbey?" She stops and looks at me. "Wanna come over tonight? I think it's a Chunky Monkey night."

I can tell she wants to ask me why, but instead she only nods before walking away.

When I open the door, Abbey is standing in her pajamas, holding her *Ten Things I Hate About You* DVD and two pints of chunky monkey against her chest.

"I've got the goods." She grins.

Taking one of the pints of ice cream, I laugh. "You're the greatest!" I respond thankfully.

We both shuffle our way over to my couch, each of us grabbing one of the spoons I laid out on the coffee table in preparation for this event. I stick the DVD in and take a seat on the couch next to Abbey.

Each of us opening our Chunky Monkey, we start eating without saying another word.

About halfway through my pint and one-third of the way through the movie, I can't hold it in any longer. "He's on a date," I say as I take another huge bite, thankful it's one full of the right combination of chocolate, banana, and nuts.

Although I don't look at her, instead keeping my eyes on the movie, I know she doesn't look at me either. She takes another bite of her ice cream. Abbey's thinking, searching for the right words, so she can make her point honestly without hurting my feelings. When she still doesn't say anything, I can't wait any longer.

"Abbey, did you hear me? Drew is on a date. We are sleeping together, and I'm eating Chunky Monkey, my thighs growing, and he's on a date." I shove another bite into my mouth. I grimace when I can't taste any banana chunks in it.

She still says nothing. Abbey just keeps eating her ice cream and watching Heath Ledger charm Julia Stiles with his bad-boy reputation and Australian accent.

Releasing a loud sigh, I admit reluctantly, "I'm supposed to be okay with the fact he is on a date."

Abbey must see this as a statement worthy of a response because she shouts, "Duh, Rosie!" She slaps me on the arm before continuing, "This is the deal you made. This is how casual sexy time works."

I take another bite and nod my head in agreement, even if my heart feels like it's revolting against me.

Abbey grabs my phone and starts searching through my Match.com list of matches. "Eat your Chunky Monkey and dream about..." She pauses, and I watch as she scrolls through the profiles. "Dream about Magnificent Matt and all the potential fun you will have tomorrow night. On. Your. Date," she says with emphasis, trying to remind me that I'm dating too, and this is exactly what I agreed to with Drew.

Gah, I hate when she's right.

I take the phone from her and look at the screen. She's right. Matt is nice to look at, and who knows what will come of it?

I lean over and kiss her cheek. Her attention is on the movie again, but her lips tip up at the corners. I quickly dip my spoon into her pint and pull a bite out. She tries to slap my hand, but I'm too quick. She throws a scowl at me, and I just grin. "There was a chunk of banana," I say unapologetically. Abbey rolls her eyes.

We spend the rest of the night watching teen rom coms while I silently pretend I've forgotten all about Drew and his date.

CHAPTER *Twelve*

I t's been a rough day and this date isn't going any better. I should've known something was off today with all the tension-filled conversations I've had over the last eight hours.

I look across the table at Matt, my latest online match.

The only thing I can say about Matt is at least he lets me eat and drink what I want. If I didn't have food, Matt might have ended up the victim to the raving, hangry lunatic I would surely be tonight. Instead, the delicious food and tangy wine are keeping me from punching him in the face.

I take another sip of my wine before looking around for Drew. We barely spoke before my date arrived. He only said a few words, kissed my cheek and let me know he'd be here if I needed him. I wanted to ask him again if he was alright but decided against it. Maybe he's done with our deal? The thought causes pain in my chest, but as usual, I push the thought aside.

I spot him sitting a few tables over.

As he has done every time, Drew's eyes are glued to me. I raise my eyebrow in acknowledgment, and his expression doesn't change.

When I look back over to my date, he gives me another smarmy smile.

An uncomfortable chill runs up my arms. My God he is creepy.

Something is just not right with him.

"What do you do for your workouts again? Because your body is rockin'," he asks me, his eyes roaming over every part of my body that isn't hidden by the table.

Suddenly, I jump back a little when I feel a hand move over my knee. I let out a startled yelp. From the corner of my eye, I see Drew stand up, but he doesn't move further when I pick up my purse and scoot my chair out.

"Please excuse me a moment while I go to the ladies' room," I say as I move away from the table toward the bathrooms. I don't even give my date a chance to say anything. I just walk away, never looking back.

When I reach the short hallway, I dash inside the ladies' room to escape.

I take a slow, steady breath. I'm only alone for a moment before the door is swinging open. It's Drew. I'm in his arms, and his hand is on my face before I have time to think about the fact he just entered the ladies' restroom.

Cupping my face, his thumb glides gently over my skin. It's comforting…calming, something I haven't felt all day. "Did he touch you?" he asks, a gentleness to his voice. I can't speak because I'm still trying to process the strange way he's looking at me. "Tell me, Rosie. Did he touch you?" he demands.

"Drew, barely on my knee, and it doesn't matter," I tell him.

"It matters," he states sternly. "He can't do that; it's a rule," he says irrationally. He starts placing kisses all around my mouth. "It's a rule, Rosie," he repeats in between each kiss. I close my eyes, releasing a sigh of contentment.

Finally, Drew's mouth is covering mine. The relief I feel when his lips touch mine tells me what I already knew; I've been waiting for this all day.

Suddenly, the gentle touch he started with turns into a frenzy of hands and kisses. He's touching my entire body either with his hands or his mouth. I can barely think straight.

One minute I'm standing in the middle of the ladies' room, and the next he has me pressed against the wall, his hand up my dress, leaving a yearning at my center when he suddenly pulls away. He stops kissing me, and I freeze, still panting as he silently lowers me to the ground.

His forehead pressed against mine, neither of us says a word for an undetermined amount of time.

"Jesus, Rosie. Don't ever let anyone do that to you again. Not me. Not anyone," he tells me, not moving. Then he pulls me into an embrace, his arms tight around me. "I'm going insane with want for you. God, how I want you," he breathes.

I finally say, "Me too."

"You owe this guy nothing. Leave," he tells me seriously. "Hell, you owe me nothing, but I'm going to walk out of this bathroom right now, and I'll be waiting outside your door for you. It will be your decision if you let me in or not."

Drew doesn't even give me time to say anything in response. He simply turns and walks out the door.

I stand frozen in place, unable to move because if I do, I might not be able to stand.

I don't move until two young girls walk in giggling minutes later. They smile at me, and I rush from the bathroom.

I don't return to the table, but I do go directly home.

CHAPTER Thirteen

I walk silently to my door, past Drew. He picks himself up from the floor without saying a word, keeping his head down. When I unlock the door, I walk through it and turn back to face Drew standing on the other side, his head hanging, staring down at his feet. I watch him. It's like he thinks I should punish him like he's done something wrong. He just doesn't get it.

"Are you coming in or not?" I ask, trying to keep it light. He peers at me from the tops of his eyes, a slow grin forming on his face. Abruptly, he's rushing toward me, taking me in his arms. His mouth crashes against mine, hard and fast like it's the last time he will ever kiss me. I don't like the thought, so I push it away. Pushing the door closed with his foot, he continues to kiss me, backing me up until my back hits the wall. I wrap myself around him, trying to pull him closer. We're moving again, and we don't stop until we fall onto my bed. Both of us yank at the other's clothes until we're completely bare. Drew leaves me for only a moment; I watch his every movement as he keeps his promise always to keep me safe. Then he's hovering over me again. He slowly moves his face down to mine, placing a lingering kiss on my forehead, my nose, and finally on my mouth before he rocks into me, filling me with warmth and wonder, and taking away the ache from the day.

We fit perfectly as usual, but there is something different about being with Drew this time. Drew is different. It seems every move he makes is with some sort of newfound purpose. He pulls out of me, and I want to cry out from the absence of him inside me. I don't have time because he is slowly teasing every inch of my skin. Drew is moving slowly down to my throbbing core, his breath tickling my inner thigh just before his tongue caresses my center. Pushing my hips forward, wanting him deeper, I cry out his name, "Drew!" Suddenly, he leaves me aching even more and places lingering kisses up my body until he reaches my mouth, giving me a searing kiss at the same time he moves his long, hard length into me once more.

"You taste so fucking good," he whispers against my lips. "You feel so god damn good." With each word, our movements become more feverish, and our breathing more labored. I've never felt so safe yet completely exposed and vulnerable at the same time. Drew is stripping me of all coherent and rational thought, but he's right beside me for the entire ride. We take everything from one another until there is nothing left in us to give and we are completely undone.

I've been lying in his arms while he tells me stories about his family. I smile at the image of little Drew learning to surf, scraping his knees after a skateboard accident, and gardening with his grandmother.

This is the first time he has revealed this much about himself on a more than superficial level.

I don't say much for fear he may realize he has gotten comfortable.

"Hey, did you fall asleep?" he asks me sweetly.

Shaking my head, I whisper, "Nope, just listening."

I'm trying to stay awake because I know the minute I fall asleep this moment will be over. The wall will be back up, and I will wake up alone. This is one moment in time I wish wouldn't end.

"I think I would have liked little Drew." I yawn.

I can feel him smile against my neck. Placing tiny kisses to my neck, he quietly says, "I think little Drew would've liked little Rosie. Now go to sleep."

I feel one last kiss on the top of my head before I reluctantly drift to sleep, unable to stop it.

The sunlight pours in through the windows, falling over my eyes. It burns, and I haven't even opened my eyes yet.

I'm not ready to open my eyes anyway because now that I'm awake, I need my one minute. My one minute of melancholy. I have it every morning after Drew. After the blissful night shared with him where I feel connected and whole. Forty-five seconds more, so I can wallow in pity. It helps me to put a time limit on it. Thirty seconds more to acknowledge I created this situation for myself. Fifteen seconds to frown. For a tear to slip down my cheek. Five seconds for me to wipe it away. Swallow my sorrow to open my eyes and begin another day.

Suddenly, a shadow casts over me. I can tell because the sunlight is no longer warming my skin.

"What are you doing?" He sounds anxious.

My eyes flash open in surprise. "You stayed," I breathe.

"I know, I'm so sorry. I never fall asleep. I know this wasn't part of the deal," he apologizes. That strange look of worry is clouding his features again.

"It doesn't matter," I try to tell him.

"It does matter, Rosie. It matters because I don't do this. I don't do the morning after. I've already broken so many rules. I care so much about you. You mean so much to me, but I can't…I can't do more."

Sitting up and pulling the sheet around me, I reach for him, but he flinches away from me.

"It's not that you can't. It's that you won't," I argue.

"I can't. Is it time, Rosie?" he asks a look of despair on his face.

He doesn't have to explain what he means by that because that was the other part of our deal. When it was time to walk away from this arrangement, we needed to recognize it. I'm just not sure I'm ready.

"No, it's not time," I contend. "I just…nevermind."

"You just what? I don't want to hurt you," he says, sadness tinging every word. "You have to be sure and tell me," he continues.

"I'm sure I'm not ready for this to be done yet," I state firmly. We both know that really doesn't solve the dilemma we're in right now. It leaves room for interpretation, and we both know I did that on purpose. I see it in his eyes as much as I feel it in my heart. He's going to let it slide, and I'm going to let him.

Leaning forward, he kisses me on the forehead. "I gotta go. I'll call you later."

I only nod. When he leaves the room, I sink back down onto the bed, feeling defeated. This morning I'm going to need another minute.

The Morning After

Pivotal moment number four happened five days ago. It's now known as "The Morning After." That morning changed me. More than I even realized at the time. More than I realize five days later.

CHAPTER
Fourteen

A few days have passed since I woke up, and Drew was still with me. The morning after. The time I realized that I had been hoping for something that would never transpire. The moment I knew Drew hadn't lied to me when he said he wouldn't commit. The moment I knew I'm the one who lied to both of us when I said I understood that and could handle casual sex without promises.

Now I'm sitting alone at The Roasting Company at a small table. It's splurge day, so I'm having a white chocolate mocha with extra whipped cream and reading the latest romance novel Abbey gave me.

Thank God it's funny.

Turning to the next chapter, I take a drink of my mocha and close my eyes, savoring it.

"Whatcha reading?" a familiar voice asks from behind me. I can tell he is trying to keep his tone light so we can forget the tension that has been among us for the last week.

Without saying a word, I turn the book over so he can read the title himself because I'm not sure I trust my voice right now.

He bursts into laughter. "How to Date a Douchebag: The Studying Hours. A novel by Sara Ney." He laughs even louder.

Whipping around to face him, I give him the evil eye.

That didn't stop him. "I thought I was the one giving you the how-to's on that." He grins wide.

We both explode again, laughing so hard Drew's crying.

"You really aren't that funny, you know?" I tell him between laughs.

"Then why are you laughing?" he asks, giving me a smile I love.

Before our conversation can go any further, Abbey walks up, a tall, handsome blond standing with her.

"Hey, what's happening?" She sounds overly cheerful. I notice her eyes slant toward Drew.

"Hey," I say with just as much enthusiasm. My eyes are darting between her and the guy next to her. "Nothing, just waiting for you."

"Soooo, this is Travis," she introduces the guy next to her. Again, I notice her glance at Drew. When I look at Drew briefly, he's solely focused on the guy we now know as Travis. I'd never mentioned to Drew that Abbey wanted to set me up with someone named Travis. It wasn't intentional; it just wasn't important.

I turn my attention back to them and away from Drew. Extending my hand to him, I smile. "Travis, nice to meet you. Abbey has told me so much about you."

As we shake hands, I notice the way his cheek dimples. Attractive. "It's nice to meet you too, Rosie. I ran into Abbey a few minutes ago, and she told me she was meeting you here. Since she's been wanting us to meet, I thought why not now? I hope that's okay," he explains. A rambler. Cute.

Suddenly there's another hand extended between us. My attention turns to Drew, who is now standing. His six-foot-two frame is slightly taller than Travis. At first, Travis looks startled by the intrusion. His forehead creases, then he releases my hand. Taking Drew's extended hand, he shakes it. "Uh, Travis," he says, confused.

Drew's eyes never leave Travis's face. "Drew. I've heard nothing about you, Travis."

I see Abbey's face; it turns slightly pink, and she rolls her eyes. Awkward. This is the most uncomfortable meeting ever, and that's a lot coming from the girl who often resides as the queen of awkward.

Trying to break the strain surrounding us, I stand up abruptly.

Travis pulls his hand from Drew's grasp. I hear Abbey whisper in Drew's direction, "Why don't you just take a piss on her and get it over with?"

Drew glares at her.

Dear God, I hope Travis didn't hear her.

"I know!" I exclaim a little too cheerfully. "Let's get a bigger table. Of course, I don't mind if you stay. Any friend of Abbey's is a friend of mine." Shit. Now I'm rambling, and I don't think it's making me look cute. I'm pretty sure I look crazy. Damn it; it's panic setting in.

Abbey laughs. Drew glares. Travis smiles. Someone end this misery.

Drew doesn't stay. He kisses my cheek and leaves without another word. Abbey stays all of five minutes then makes an excuse to leave.

Travis asks if I want to stay and talk. I agree. It isn't out of guilt or obligation. I genuinely would like to get to know him.

I glance at my watch and an hour has gone by. We discussed our families. He told me he grew up in San Jose, just over the hill from Santa Cruz. His parents are divorced, and he has a sister. He works for a local start-up as an engineer. He's been dating but has yet to find the girl he thinks he can take home to his mom.

Abbey was right. He's great. He's smart and kind. Good looking. He laughs a lot. Even at himself when he bungles every word out of his mouth.

It's the best hour I've spent with anyone other than Drew.

Drew. Damn Drew and his inability to commit. Damn him and his kisses and touch. Damn him.

Maybe it's time. If I want to save us, our friendship—if I want to save myself. Then maybe it's time.

I smile at Travis when I look up, and he's watching me, a sparkle of possibility in his eye. The kind of possibility of more if I wanted it.

My phone rings as soon as I walk in the door of my apartment.

"So?" Abbey squeals through the phone.

"So, what?" I reply, keeping my voice emotionless just to drive her crazy.

As glad I as I am that she introduced me to Travis, I hate the way it happened. She highjacked me. I wasn't prepared. She took me off guard. She took Drew off guard, and if I didn't know better, I'd say she enjoyed it.

"Rose Marie Fisher, I'd slap you silly if I were standing there with you! You know exactly what I'm referring to...Travis! What do you think of Travis?" She sounds like she is about to come through the phone.

I walk over to my couch and fall back onto it with a sigh.

"Travis is...Travis is amazing. He's everything you said he is, and we're going out tomorrow," I tell her.

I thought I'd hear her scream with excitement, but her voice is scolding.

"Then why do you sound like your family pet just died?" she asks me, a tinge of annoyance echoing through the phone.

"I do not!" I debate.

"You do, and I want to know why!" she says, frustration hanging on her words.

"Because I think Drew is upset. Abbey, his face. Things have been weird between us this week and for some reason, I think the idea of Travis hurts him. I don't want to hurt him, Abbey," I try to explain to her.

She's silent for a long time. I wait because I know she has something to say. I wait because I'm afraid to say anything else.

"Rosie, I've wanted to say this for a while. I like Drew. A lot. He's great. Great looking. A great friend. And by the look on your face most days, great in bed. But that's it. He won't commit. He can't do more, and as much as you try to tell yourself you've changed, you haven't. You, Rosie Fisher, are a more kind of girl. It's time to recognize it and see there is someone who can be all those things and more for you."

Tears slide down my cheeks. A loud sob escapes me and echoes through the phone.

"Damn it, Rosie. I'm sorry. I didn't mean…" Abbey apologizes.

"No, you're right. I know you're right. It doesn't make it any easier." I sigh between hiccups through the phone. "I know what I have to do."

CHAPTER *Fifteen*

I asked Drew to meet me near the lighthouse. I figured somewhere private, but at the same time public, would keep me from changing my mind. Because I know the minute I see him, the temptation will be almost unbearable.

There's a light breeze coming off the ocean, which is normal for this time of day. The evenings are always cooler. I pull my sweater tight around me, trying to trap some of the heat.

A few surfers are taking the last set of waves just before the sun goes down. It's peaceful to watch, even with the storm brewing inside me.

My hands are resting on the railing. Overlooking the cliff, I close my eyes and release a deep sigh.

"It's not time." He sounds sad. I didn't even hear him walk up.

"Drew…"

"No, Rosie." He takes me by the shoulders, turning me so I'm facing him. "No, Rosie," he repeats.

I close my eyes again because I can't look at him.

"God, Drew…" I sigh. It takes everything in me to keep the tears from falling.

"Damn it, Rosie. It's not fucking time," he begs me. "Open your eyes! Look at me!"

Drew is beginning to shout, and his grip is tightening on my shoulders. I open my eyes, and the tears fall. The tears I've been holding back stream down my cheeks.

Shaking my head, I try to say what won't come out of my mouth. Why is it so damn hard to say? We promised, and he's not keeping his end of the bargain.

"Why are you doing this? You promised! You made me swear I would tell you when our arrangement got too hard. I'm trying to tell you, and you won't let me." I sob and his face twists in pain.

Pulling me against his chest, Drew wraps his arms around me.

"It's so hard, Drew. It's too hard now. It's time. My time is up," I cry, the pain of my heart hugging every word that leaves me.

He squeezes tighter. "It'll be harder when there's no us," he says tearfully.

Pushing against his chest so I can look at him, I say to him, "I need more." All the tears have suddenly ceased. "I've been falling slowly…so very slowly in love with you. I want more."

His eyes are shining with his own unshed tears, and he groans. "I can't do more."

Resigned, I give him a sad smile. "I know, and that's why it's time."

Rising to my tiptoes as he lowers his head, our lips press lightly together. I feel a tear hit my face. One that isn't mine. We linger that way, neither taking the kiss deeper nor pulling apart.

Just savoring the touch, the feeling of perfection, of our last kiss.

My heart is splitting. I need to leave. Gradually, I pull my lips from his.

As I take a step backward, a quiet plea leaves him. "Please…."

I stand there in front of him, wearing my heart on my sleeve, waiting for him to continue. When it finally becomes obvious he isn't going to say more, I shrug, wipe the tears from my cheeks, push my shoulders back, and turn. I walk away. I don't look back. Not even when I hear him say, "Don't leave me." I can't.

Not even when I feel my heart stay with him.

It's been two weeks since I kissed Drew goodbye. We've stayed friends, but it's still new. Raw. So we've seen very little of one another. I can tell the change of our relationship has affected our entire coffee shop family.

Lenny, Marti, Colleen, and Lorna tiptoe around the subject of Drew. Although not one of them knows the true nature of what transpired between us, they know something was happening between us.

Lynn has been extra attentive. He's spent extra time trying to make me smile.

As for Andy, he keeps quiet. He carried on as if nothing ever changed. In a way, for him, it didn't because not once in all the months Drew and I became more than friends but less than committed, did Andy ever change his behavior toward us. It's almost like he knew Drew and I were having our "moment in time" he always seems to be living.

I've seen quite a bit of Travis, although we've been taking things slow. He's been wonderful about respecting my wishes. Abbey is happy about the progress I've been making with Travis, but she keeps her excitement to a minimum because she knows I'm still hurting over Drew.

I recognize I'm feeling better and better as the days pass, but I find myself having a setback on the days I see him.

As for Drew, he seems to be handling things well. I try not to wonder about who he's seeing or how many girls he takes out. I just try to see Drew as I did before the arrangement.

I'm moving on, and I'm sure he is too.

Travis and I walk into the Crow's Nest holding hands. Tonight there's music outside on the beach; I can hear it drifting into the restaurant through the open doors. We decide to order a drink and take them outside so we can hear the music better.

I don't see him at first as we walk up to the bar until we are standing next to him.

Then it's like I can notice no one else. Drew stands and indicates for me to take his seat.

I feel Travis's hand tighten on mine. "Ah, thanks, man, but we're just going to order a couple of drinks and take them outside," he says with an edge to his friendliness.

Drew doesn't even look at Travis. Doesn't acknowledge him. He only looks at me. I've seen this look a hundred times; it's always confused me, but for some reason tonight I feel more confused than ever.

I feel my heart rate speed up.

Finally, I break free of his stare and say, "No, thank you, Drew. I'm good. Like Travis said, we're just going to grab some drinks and go outside to listen to the music." Damn it; I'm talking too much because I'm nervous when a simple no would have been sufficient. And Drew will know that…he knows me.

"You're adorable," he says as if he is oblivious to the presence of Travis or my words.

Travis takes a step toward me, and his grip tightens on my hand. "Ouch," I say involuntarily. It hurt even though he did it unintentionally.

Travis looks down at me, an apology in his eyes. "I'm sorry," he says sincerely.

Drew pulls my other hand, yanking me from Travis's loosened grip, and behind him. "Drew!" I shout as Travis steps toward us, bowing his chest.

I push Drew to the side and step between them. "Travis, let's just go outside. We can order from the waitress out there," I plead with him. He looks down at me and nods his head.

He takes me by the hand and begins to lead me away, but I stop, holding up one finger, indicating I need a minute. He nods reluctantly.

I turn back to Drew, who is still standing there staring at us.

"What are you doing, Drew? You can't do that, okay?" I wait for him to answer me. To give me any indication he gets what I'm saying. I've never seen him so emotionless. I pull his gaze to mine, and when I touch his face, I feel him tremble. When he's looking at me, I ask him again, "Okay?"

He doesn't move. He only stares. If he didn't blink, I would almost wonder if he fell asleep with his eyes open. His eyes start moving, looking into mine like he's searching for an answer to a question he hasn't even asked me yet.

Damn it, Drew. I don't have any answers. The only answer I had, I gave you.

Without a word, he nods at me, turns around, and sits back down at the bar in his same chair. I stand there staring at his back until I feel a tug on my hand. Looking over my shoulder, I see a waiting Travis.

"You ready?" is all he asks. He makes no demands. He doesn't get angry. Travis just simply asks if I'm ready. He wants to get away from Drew and go out to the patio. The weight of that simple question is more than he realizes. I'm supposed to walk away from Drew and be with him. The funny thing is, if I'm honest, I really don't think I am ready to answer that.

CHAPTER *Sixteen*

I t's an hour or so later before I see Drew again.

I didn't stop thinking about him. Rather I decided to focus on Travis. Then suddenly there he is, leaning against the wall, watching me. It reminds me of all the times I would be on dates, and he would be watching. Waiting for me to need him. Waiting for the guy to screw up. Just watching and waiting for me to meet him back at my apartment.

I frown when I think about the fact that can't happen anymore.

He can't wait for me because I won't need him. This guy, Travis, he won't screw up. I can't stop him from watching me, but there is no need for him to wait. I don't need him anymore. I won't ask him to go to my apartment. I won't let him in. It strikes me as I watch him now, watching me, that ironically I always let him in, but the problem was he never really let me in.

Travis pulls me closer, and I rest my head on his chest. I allow him to wrap his arms tighter around me. I hear his heartbeat, and I'm trying to connect with it. I want to be familiar with its tune. I'm desperate for it. I don't.

He's too close. I'm still too aware of him. I can still feel his eyes on me from across the patio, staring, caressing every part of me with familiarity as his gaze roams over my body.

What is he doing? I'm with someone else. He needs to stop. I swiftly glance in his direction, telling him with this single look how I feel about the way he's acting. He's giving my date the wrong impression. Drew doesn't own me, but you wouldn't know it by the possessive way he took my hand earlier. He doesn't even flinch away from the daggers I'm throwing with my eyes. Drew doesn't even blink. His gaze seems only to get more possessive, especially when Travis's hand moves lower down my back.

I like Travis. Travis likes me. I can have more with Travis. The kind of more I can't have with Drew. He made it clear from the beginning. He said it over and over until I had no choice but to believe him.

"Are you having a good time?" Travis whispers in my ear as we turn in slow circles.

His question pulls me from my thoughts of Drew.

Pulling back so I can look him in the eyes, I smile. "Yes, thank you."

"Good, because I really like you, Rosie," he confesses, looking down into my eyes. I can tell he means it. I lay my head on his shoulder, and we continue to sway to the music. I feel his arms tighten a little more around me, and his hands go a little lower.

Within seconds, I'm being pulled from his arms.

"What the hell, man?" Travis questions. I can hear the shock and anger in his voice.

"Get your fucking hands off of her!" Drew roars.

Travis's eyes widen, and I'm standing, my body against Drew's chest, his hand still firmly wrapped around my wrist. I don't move. My surprised gaze is bouncing between them. I can feel Drew's chest moving up and down, the tension moving beneath his skin. I still can't move.

"Is there something I should know?" Travis asks.

I seem to pull myself out of my confused haze. "No," I say, pushing at Drew's chest.

"Yes," Drew says at the same time, tightening his grip and holding me against him.

Travis watches the way Drew cradles me against him.

"Which is it, yes or no?"

I look up at Drew pleadingly, but I'm struck by the fact he is giving me the same desperate, pleading look. What is he doing? Why?

"Rosie..." Travis says my name, trailing off, sounding defeated. I look back at him.

"Drew, let me go!" I demand with as much conviction as I can muster. His grip loosens and reluctantly, he lets me go completely. Turning, I face away from him and look at my date. "Travis, I need to speak with Drew. Alone. I'm so sorry."

He winces.

"I think maybe I should go," he tells me, the gentleness of his voice from earlier gone.

Reaching out to him as he turns away, I put my hand on his arm. "No, I only need a minute."

Looking back at me and then over my shoulder at Drew, who I can still feel standing close behind me, he shakes his head.

"No, you don't. I'm going to go. Call me when you're ready." He leans forward and places a kiss on my lips. Drew steps closer to me and tenses; I can feel his body against mine.

"Okay, I'll call you tomorrow, and Travis, I'm so, so sorry," I choke out.

He walks away without looking back. I watch him until he's out of my sight and even after because I'm not ready to turn around and face Drew quite yet.

Without looking back, I start walking toward the door, going to the one place we will have privacy. I don't even look back at Drew, but I know he's following me.

Walking out into the night air and several doors down, I can see there is one remaining light on in the coffee house. Andy works tonight, so I knock on the window.

His face suddenly appears, a smile crossing his features when he recognizes the two of us staring back at him. I still haven't looked at or spoken to Drew.

"Hello, you two. What brings you by here at this hour?" Andy says cheerfully, not noticing the thick tension surrounding us.

"Hi, Andy, I know you're closing, but could Drew and I possibly come in for a few minutes? We need a place to talk," I ask, trying not to give my mood away.

"Absolutely. I was about to walk out back, but if you want, I'll just lock up and let you guys close the doors behind you," he tells us, a slightly concerned look crossing his features. In typical Andy fashion, he doesn't intrude.

I lean forward and place a kiss on his cheek as I pass him.

"Andy," Drew says as he walks by him. "Thank you."

Andy gives Drew the nod. "Anything for my two favorite customers."

Just as he said, Andy locks the doors and walks out the back without another word. My back is still to Drew, and when I whip around to face him, he's standing before me, arms at his side, looking tormented. Our eyes meet, so familiar. So sad. So goddamn beautiful. I want to know what the hell has gotten into him. I'm so angry. Hurt. I need to know why he's acting like such an ass.

"Drew, what the hell was all of that?" I ask him in anger, taking a step closer to him. Andy didn't hesitate to leave us alone, so when the words leave my mouth, his eyes grow apologetic and wide. There is something in their depths I've never seen before, and I don't know how to react. He looks as if he doesn't know how to answer me. I wait for him to speak, but he remains silent. Drew only stares at me with those piercing blue eyes.

Finally, he starts to say something, and I wait for his answer to my question. The answer never comes.

"When did it get so hard to breathe around you?" he asks me.

I feel like my heart stops. Time freezes after this one simple statement. I'm baffled by what he says. The confusion is dissipating my fury.

"I don't know what you mean," I claim, my voice barely a whisper.

"Damn it, Rosie. This wasn't what I intended to happen. I don't do this." He waves his hand between us. "This doesn't happen to me. I have everything I want. I don't want more... I didn't want more." I flinch because now Drew sounds irritated and he's rambling.

"Drew, I...I don't know what you're saying. This is exactly what was supposed happen. This was our plan...our deal," I beg, yet I have no idea what I'm begging for.

"No!" He runs a hand through his hair and over his face. "No, you're wrong. This isn't what we planned. This isn't the deal I made. My life was supposed to stay controlled. I was supposed to walk away, and my life was supposed to continue turning on its normal axis, but then..."

He pauses, sitting down in the one chair left in the coffee shop that isn't turned upside down on a table. His elbows are resting on his knees, his face in his hands. I remain frozen, unable to move or think or speak. This isn't the cool, calm, and confident Drew I know.

This Drew is scaring me. He sounds sad. This guy is saying things I can't wrap my mind around because these words are not the words of my Drew. My Drew? He isn't my Drew. I continue silently watching him. Minutes pass and nothing. Once more, I'm feeling the need to fill the silence that is hanging in the air around us.

"Drew, I..." I say in a whisper, just loud enough to be heard.

Abruptly, he stands, interrupting me.

"Don't, Rosie." His voice is off. He turns away from me. "You have no idea." He laughs, but it isn't the laugh I'm used to hearing. This one sounds dejected. I don't like it. I need to see his face. I step toward him even though I promised myself I wouldn't touch him again in anything but friendship. I wouldn't touch him at all. I'm breaking that promise now. When I lay my hand on his shoulder, a shudder runs through his body; I can feel it move through mine.

Before I can say anything, he begins to speak again. "You wanted me to teach you to be more confident. To be a person who is noticed. The ironic thing is, Rosie..." He swivels back around to face me and my hand falls to my side. "The most laughable thing is you were always noticeable. From the moment I saw you dashing down the side-walk in the rain, I knew it. When I caught you in my arms and peered into your whiskey-colored eyes, I was sure of it."

I want to stop him, but the words won't come out. He needs to stop. I need him to stop, but he keeps going. He's standing so close, and the more he says, the harder it is for me to breathe.

"I've never met anyone who only had to walk into a room to so naturally and unintentionally command the attention of everyone in it. You touch people with a simple glance. They fall more under your spell with every awkward word that slips past your lips. I know I did. This is why I should've known when you asked me to be a part of this charade, I should've turned you down. That the moment I touched you, I mean really touched you, I would be ruined forever.

But I was cocky. Arrogant. I made the stupid mistake of pretend-ing you were like any other girl. The mistake of pretending I could walk away from this unchanged and back to my old life."

I'm shaking now. I can't hear any more. He's right. This wasn't supposed to happen. Drew was supposed to walk away, and I was sup-posed to be happy and confident. I knew he could never truly want someone like me. Someone like Drew Nallen would never want the scattered, naïve, or plain Rosie Fisher.

"I think I fell...I think I may want more," he finally says, pulling my attention back to him. One word has me stepping back and keeping my distance. Think. He almost had me until he said the word *think*.

Now I let out a long and boisterous laugh. It sounds just as off as Drew's did moments ago. "You think? Did you just end all of that with you *think* you may want more?" I shout at him, pronouncing each word he just said back to him. I'm pissed again. Hurt. Scared. His expression changes and I can tell I've shocked him. He wasn't expecting me to get angry. Why am I angry?

"Rosie, that's not..." he begins to say.

"Oh, that's not what you meant?" I spit out at him as he shakes his head. He looks like he is about to speak again, but I put my hand up. I push down every feeling I can feel pumping through my heart in the excitement of what the implications of his words mean. I shove them so far down until I'm sure they can't leak out.

"You're wrong," I state. "You're so very wrong. This was the exact purpose of our deal. I'm smarter about relationships. I'm more confident in who I am…more experienced." I try not to think of Drew's lips running over my body. "You were supposed to get your kicks and walk away, back to your fun, uncommitted bachelor life. You told me I couldn't want more and I held up our end of the bargain."

He reaches for me, but I move out of his reach. He takes two more steps toward me, but he keeps his hands at his side. "You don't mean this…you have to know."

"I do mean it," I argue.

"I won't accept it," he insists, an edge to his voice.

I smile a sad smile and lift my hand, placing it on the side of his cheek.

"We were never meant to be more than this. Accept it, Drew." I swallow the thick knot that has formed in my throat. "I have," I barely choke out.

I drop my hand and brush past him, leaving Drew Nallen standing alone in the barely lit room where we first met. I know better than to look back because if I do, he may charm me into staying. He may convince me his words are as real as he has convinced himself. Then he would eventually realize he didn't mean what he's saying now. He'd leave me, and I'd never recover.

So it's simple; I'm leaving him first before he has a chance to destroy me.

When I Walked Away

Pivotal moment number five happened the day I listened to my head instead of my heart.

My head will protect me.
My heart will break me.

Epilogue

Drew

I was in the middle before I even knew it began.

"Damn it!" I yell, my words echoing off the brick walls of the empty coffee shop, bouncing back at me and hitting me directly in the gut. I bend over at the waist, trying to hold myself together. The ache. The painful realization that I screwed up. Fuck, I don't know how this happened. I never saw her coming.

You know those dreams you might have when you're younger? Maybe you're at a carnival. Maybe in a park with your mom or family. A dream where you're walking along, enjoying yourself, no cares, no worries, only thinking about what makes you happy. Then suddenly, without warning, you're at the edge of a cliff, and before you realize what is happening, you're free falling.

Falling so fast. You can see the ground getting closer. You're scared because you have no idea how this will end. So many things could happen… good, bad, but it's completely out of your control. That is where I am.

I'm free falling.

I've spent most of my twenties trying to avoid any kind of relationship with expectations or real commitment. I liked my life that way, and six months ago, I had no plans of it changing. Then I met Rose Fisher. Rosie. Sweet smile. Long, toned legs. Natural, awkward as hell, Rosie.

Yep, I went free falling head first in love with Rosie Fisher.

I may not know how I'm going to handle this whole being in love thing, but I sure as hell will not be going down without a fight. Because I know, no matter what she says, she's in love with me. We're free falling together. She just won't let herself see it. She's scared, and God damn it, that's my fault because I'm the one who put that fear in there. I fueled it every time I told her I couldn't do more.

I'm going to prove to her I was wrong. I was so wrong because more is all I want with her.

After I knock on her door for the third time, I finally hear a sound on the other side. The door opens, and there is Rosie, staring up at me, bleary eyed and, well, a completely beautiful mess.

I planned what I would say to her the whole way over here, and now I've got nothing. Not one eloquent or romantic word to convince her to give me a chance. Not a single one.

"Drew," she says, a touch of anger hugging her words.

Her eyes tell me more. They always have. They hold the secrets she wants to stay hidden. I want to reach out and touch her. Feel her soft, smooth skin beneath my fingertips. I want to press my lips against hers, beg her with a kiss to forgive me. Believe me. Love me.

I look at the floor, trying to find my balance.

Fuck. I'm a goner.

Running a hand through my hair, I glance at her from the tops of my eyes before I stutter out the first words that come to my mind. "Look what you've done to me."

She laughs; it's almost maniacal. She keeps laughing until suddenly she's not laughing. *Please laugh, Rosie.* I want her to laugh; I don't care how crazy it sounds. Because now that she's not laughing, she's crying. Then she's not.

Rosie takes a step back, opening the door wider in what I assume is an invitation to come inside her apartment. She's letting me in. A spark of hope ignites. As I walk past her, I realize she may be letting me in her house, but that doesn't mean she's letting me back in for good.

She can't.

Be sure to continue to read
Rosie and Drew's story,
told in Drew's POV.

Free Falling

free FALLING

To anyone trying
to protect their heart.

The risk is worth it.

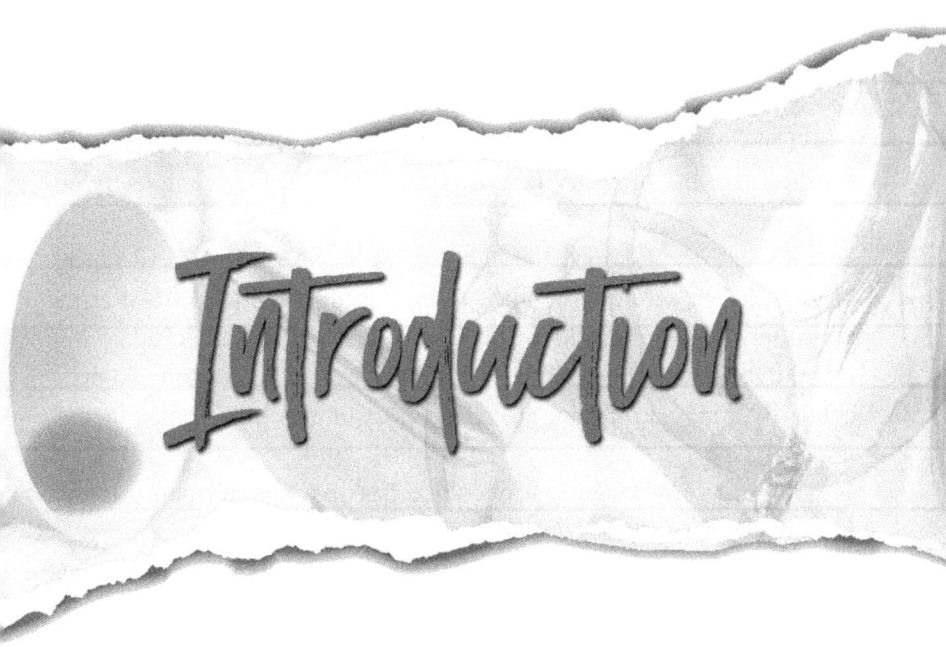

Introduction

Hello, I'm Andrew Thomas Nallen. My mom has always called me Andrew, but everyone else I know calls me Drew. My life has been pretty easy. I come from a good, loving family. I have a great job. I've had my whole life planned out since I was nineteen. That was the year I changed. The year I had my heart broken. The year I realized I never wanted to lose myself in anyone or anything again. Everyone who knows me understands I like to be in control of my life. Don't get me wrong. I have feelings. I love my family. I love my friends. I love my job. But, none of those control my life. I control my life. My mom is constantly worrying I'm always going to be alone. The thing she doesn't understand is I'm never alone. I enjoy life. I'm social. I live the way I want to live, and I'm happy. I just choose to never get too close.

I got close once. Laura had me. Then Laura did the unthinkable. I was crushed at the ripe age of nineteen. It was brutal, and I swore I'd never do brutal again. After Laura, I avoided relationships and commitments at all costs. I became what some might call a playboy. The one disappointment of my mom's life. She could never understand why I built my wall so high. And boy was it high. So high that it stood tall for ten years without any threat of coming down. It was solid. Indestructible.

Until Rosie.

The right thing to say is I used to never to get too close. Because for the first time in nearly ten years, my life is feeling completely out of control.

Rosie Fisher slipped through a crack in my wall. Picked up my heart and then carefully climbed to the top of it until we stood at the very top and she plunged us both head-first off the other side. Now we're free falling. Free falling so fast, it's impossible to stop. No parachute. No rope. Head first into all the possibilities love brings, including heartache.

I heard somewhere that everyone has five pivotal moments that can change the course of their life and lead them in the direction of their fate. I never believed this until these moments of time were set into motion in my life.

They all began with Rosie Fisher. She changed everything. She changed me.

Today, I'm free falling into love.

Prologue

Rosie

The moment I said the words, I wanted to take them back. I wish I could, but I know I can't. It's impossible.

I walk quickly out the door and lean against the cold brick of the building. The fog has come in, and it's hanging on every street-light down the avenue. I feel as if I just ran a marathon; it's hard to breathe.

I just walked away from Drew Nallen like the words he said meant nothing. It didn't matter he said he thought he was falling for me. Or that he thought he wanted to try for something more. None of it matters because he still didn't sound sure. He sounded uncertain. And I deserve more than reluctance. At least, I told myself the words didn't matter. But…

It's not true. They do mean something, but my heart can't trust exactly what and for how long. It's Drew. Sexy, charming, and self-assured, he captured every part of me, and I let him. I trusted him. I still trust him. I just don't trust his heart or mine.

I shut my eyes tight and place my hands over my ears when I hear

Drew's words echo through the coffee shop. It isn't loud out here, but the anguish I hear in his voice makes me want to run back into the building and take a chance. I have to get out of here.

Pushing away from the wall, I make my way toward my apartment.

I don't stop until I reach my front door. Not when Abbey calls and not even when she calls again. I open the door, walk in, and shut it immediately. I drop everything I'm holding and move directly to the couch, falling onto it, curling into the fetal position, and allowing the tears to flow.

I'm not sure how long I lie there, crying for all the possibilities with Drew that will never be realized. My heart breaks for every maybe we were never supposed to want because that was the deal. It's not Drew.

Suddenly, a knock echoes through my apartment. I don't move at first. I don't want to, but then some feeling I have lifts me off the couch.

After the second knock, I reach the door and peer into the peephole. It's him. He's shuffling from one foot to the other. He looks desperate. I've never seen him look so desperate. Anguished. Dammit, Drew. He knocks again, this time a little harder. A little louder.

I wipe the tears from my cheeks, realizing I won't be able to hide them, but I don't really care.

Opening the door, I startle him. His face seems pale, which is odd with his olive complexion. His blue eyes are lighter than I've ever seen, but the whites of his eyes are tinged pink with sadness. Neither of us says a word. We only stare until I can't take it anymore.

"Drew," I say, allowing more of the anger I feel over the situation we put ourselves into seep into my voice.

He again just watches me. His eyes connect with mine and hold there. Then they're roaming over my face and down my body. It's like he's trying to feel me, but he doesn't reach out. His eyes are vulnerable and open. He always had that wall up, and now it's like he's suddenly allowing me over it. A chill runs up my spine.

He's searching for words. I want to tell him they won't work. His words won't work.

He runs his hand over his hair and suddenly, he stutters out, "Look what you've done to me."

What the fuck? Look what I've done to him?

The idea I'm the one who did this to him makes me feel hysterical. Manic. So I do what any sane person would do: I laugh. But it's not just any laugh. A long, drawn-out, unstable-sounding laugh. Tears threaten to fall. I feel like I might choke on them because I won't give him my tears. He isn't allowed to see them. So I laugh like a crazy person. Then I abruptly stop. The laugh won't come out anymore. I just stop. Because God damn it, the tears won this battle, and now they're streaming down my cheeks. It's like I don't want to go down without one final fight, and I block the next wave of tears from falling.

Taking a step back, I allow Drew to come in. I don't know what we'll say. I'm not sure what's left for us to say to one another, but I'll give him his chance to speak. Closure. I can see in his eyes the moment he feels hope, and then the moment he realizes I can't.

Pivotal moment number one...

Pivotal moment number one happened one rainy day...

A flash of red catches my attention as I stop a few feet from the entrance to The Roasting Company just under a small overhang to shake off my umbrella. I'm here for my daily cup of coffee. I never start my day without it.

My gaze fixates on the girl dashing across the street in the rain. I smile because she's drenched, yet while she runs across the street it appears she just looked up at the red brick building as if she's sightseeing. My eyes travel from her long, dark chocolate hair clinging to her head and face down to her short skirt over her long, tone, exposed legs to the simple ballet flats she is wearing on her feet. Her look is simple, but something stirs inside me.

As she steps up onto the curb and scurries past, she doesn't even notice me.

I definitely notice her. Her face is sweet, pure. I want to get a better look, but she keeps moving. My eyes continue to follow her and so do I. I watch as she reaches out for the door, but before she can take hold of it, her feet come out from under her. Without hesitation, I rush forward just in time for her to fall *against me.*

She releases a small, ladylike squeak as her body falls against mine.

I watch her face briefly, her eyes clenched tightly, her nose scrunched up as she was preparing for an impact that never came. Her eyes rapidly blink open once she realizes she hasn't actually fallen to the wet ground. When they finally open all the way, I feel like I'm the one who fell and made an impact with the hard ground because I feel completely out of breath as I gaze into the most amazing and unique pair of whiskey-colored eyes I've ever seen. Her cheeks begin to color, and it only enhances the beauty of her skin.

She is breathtaking. Literally.

I realize I'm still holding her, and neither of us has said a word. Barely finding my voice, I ask, "Are you alright?"

We stare into one another's eyes for another second before she smiles brightly. In that instant, I realize I'm the one who may not be alright again.

CHAPTER One

Two days after she walked away...

With my head down and my eyes focused on the cup of coffee in front of me, I miss the moment she walks in the door. My attention is only captured when I hear Lynn announce her name to the coffee shop like he's done so many times before.

I glance over the faces waiting in line, searching for hers.

I can't help myself even though I know it will hurt. She said to give her time but never said what she needs time to do. I still can't believe I'm in this position. Me? Drew Nallen, known playboy. The guy who doesn't commit. The guy who's not only in control of his life but also his heart. I never got too close. Until Rosie.

Suddenly, my eyes land on the beautiful, smooth skin of the face I was seeking. God, what I wouldn't do to touch her. Her head is turned slightly away from me. She keeps looking down at her phone. She doesn't seem like herself. The glow is gone. When she looks back up, her head turns, and our eyes lock. Even from here I can see her suck in a breath. She grimaces in what looks like pain, but she quickly pushes it away. She doesn't look away though. It's as if she physically can't. I get it because neither can I.

Before I know what I'm doing, I stand and wind through the tables toward her. The world seems to be in slow motion, and I can't reach her fast enough. What will I say? What will I do? I have no idea, but I can't stay away from her. Surprising me, Rosie begins moving in my direction like she has no control over the decision. We don't stop until we are mere inches apart. Toe to toe. Our breath mixes between us. Our scrutiny is begging the other to speak first.

I want to kiss her. I want to feel my lips against her soft ones. I want us to be alone instead of in the middle of this busy coffee shop. I want so much, but we aren't alone. And I told her I would give her space. I told her I wouldn't make this harder for her than I already have. I told her all of these things, and she asked me for all of these things, yet she's standing here before me. So close.

Involuntarily, I begin to lean toward her. Her eyes widen. She's scared. God damn it. Rosie's scared because she thinks I'm going to kiss her. And shit, I *was* going to kiss her. In that split second, I decide a change of course, one almost as good. A safer choice for both of us. I lean forward, and I gently but firmly wrap my arms around her, pulling her softly against me. She comes willingly, only hesitating a moment before hugging me back. We both release the breath we've been holding since our eyes met. Probably the same breath we've been holding since we last saw one another.

She whispers my name against my shoulder, "Drew."

"Rosie, I don't know how to make this better," I concede quietly.

Pulling slowly away from me, I reluctantly let her. Rosie looks up at me, a glossy look to her eyes from unshed tears. "I don't know either. This thing between us scares me," she admits. I nod in acknowledgment because what else can I do? It scares me too.

Behind us, her name and drink are called out by the barista, indicating her order is ready.

Rosie releases the light grasp she has on my arms and steps back. "I'll be seeing you," she mutters before turning away from me. I remain frozen in place, watching her until she leaves.

When I walk into my parents' house later this afternoon, Rosie is still fresh on my mind. I've spent most of the day trying to forget what it felt like to hold her again for those few brief seconds. Today is my brother Parker's birthday, so in our typical family tradition, we're all gathering at my parents' to celebrate. This will be good for me—help gets my mind off Rosie and our relationship.

Our.

Relationship.

My family would have a field day if they knew I had a relationship with anyone other than them and my childhood pals. Let alone, one I'm worried about it. I don't worry. I never allow myself close enough to worry.

Laughter drifts through the house from the back deck, putting a smile on my face.

When I make my way out the back door, I take in the scene before me. My mom is sitting on my dad's lap laughing, slapping at his arm that is wrapped around her waist with one hand while holding a platter of fruit with the other. I watch my sister Kelsea roll her eyes as she takes the platter from my mom. Ty and Jasper are too busy stuffing their faces with fish tacos to pay attention to anything else. My eyes finally fall onto Parker at the same time he notices me. He nods when I reach him, and I pat him on the back. "Happy birthday, big brother," I tell him.

My mom notices me and finally pulls out of my dad's grasp, making her way to me. "Oh, Andrew," she exclaims as she hugs me. "When did you get here?"

I squeeze her back, acknowledging my dad over her shoulder. "Hey, Mom, I just walked in, and it looks like the party started without me," I tease. She swats me on the arm affectionately. "You're late!" I laugh, and it feels good. I haven't had much to laugh at lately.

As soon as the thought crosses my mind, I think of Rosie.

I wonder what she's doing. I think about how nice it would be if she were here. My heart sinks again at the thought of how we left things today. A frown forms on my face when I realize nothing has changed since our talk a few days earlier. I don't have Rosie anymore. If I'm honest, I never really did, but I only have myself to blame. I'm the one who put the wall between us.

Snapping out of my thoughts, I hear Jasper asking Mom when it's time for cake, only to see her throw her momma daggers in his direction. I watch them and glance around the porch at the rest of the group. All of them in are their usual family mode, everything perfectly the same, except it's not. Everything feels different. They just have no idea. Just as I'm about to grab a plate off the table, my eyes land on the one person who knows me best: Parker. And he isn't paying attention to the argument over who gets the first slice of his cake. He's staring directly at me, a concerned look on his face. He raises one eyebrow, lifting it higher when our eyes meet. I shrug and shake my head. In typical Parker fashion, he lets it go…for now.

"Drew, how's that new project you've been working on?" my dad asks when I take a seat next to him.

For the first time since I walked through the door, Tyler decides to speak. "Yeah, Drew…what's her name this week?"

"Shut the fuck up, Ty! You have no idea what you're talking about!" I yell so loud, my voice is quivering. My family goes silent around me. I know I just overreacted. Tyler didn't say anything we wouldn't normally say to one another. It's the way we all work together. Giving one another shit and razzing one another while my dad laughs at our stupidity and my mother rolls her eyes.

But today is different. Because of Rosie. Today is different because I know normally he'd be right and that's the reason Rosie doesn't trust my feelings for her. It's the reason I'm not worthy of her.

Fuck.

I place my plate on the table and run my hand through my hair.

My dad breaks the silence. "Son?"

Lifting my gaze to my brother, I apologize. "Sorry, Ty. Bad week." Tyler nods at me. The awkward tension surrounding my family and me remains for a few moments longer until Parker breaks it.

"So, when do I open presents? There better be a lot. You guys owe me," he says. Our attention turns to Parker, and just like that, Parker in his usual way puts everything back in its right place.

"I didn't get you shit. I came for the food," Jasper says just before he stuffs another bite into his mouth. A wide, full smile crosses his face. We all roll our eyes. Jasper is the youngest in the family. He's a twenty-two-year-old recent college grad, and the only one of us who took after my mom with the blond hair and green eyes.

"Parks," I say as I reach into my pocket and pull out a twenty-dollar bill. "Happy birthday, bro." I hear my dad and Jasper laugh quietly from either side of me. Kelsea rolls her eyes and places a wrapped box on the table. "Here. If you don't like it, too bad," she tells Parker. Tyler shrugs his shoulders when Parker looks over at him.

My mom stands up and walks into the house briefly, coming back with a birthday bag as Parker tears into Kelsea's gift to him.

He pulls out a navy blue O'Neill sweatshirt and gives her a hang loose gesture. Kelsea smiles.

Mom hands him his gift, and he opens it and smiles because, as usual, my mom baked him chocolate chip banana bread and gave him gift cards to three of his favorite local restaurants. She's always trying to feed us now that we're not all at home anymore.

We all sing "Happy Birthday," eat cake, and laugh. Rosie's still in the back of my mind, but for the first time all week I'm feeling pretty good.

CHAPTER Two

A week later, I'm sitting on my couch, flipping through the channels when a loud knock echoes through my studio. I close my eyes and debate whether I want to ignore it or answer it. The longer I stay on the couch, weighing my choices, the more persistent the knock becomes, and I realize my choice has been made for me.

Standing up, I toss the remote onto the sofa as I walk away, but it bounces off and clatters to the floor.

As I shuffle to the door, the knocks come in shorter, harder, like the person on the other side is getting more annoyed with the fact I haven't answered yet. "God damn it, Drew! I hear you in there, so open the damn door," Parker's voice roars through the cracks of the doorway. "I'm not leaving," he continues.

Pulling the door open silently, I turn back for the sofa immediately without saying a word to my brother. I don't even look at him. I may have let him in, but I'm really not in the mood to talk. I hear him close the door behind me as I bend over to pick up the remote and flop back onto the couch.

"Jesus, Drew." Parker sounds exasperated and confused. "What's gotten into you? Mom says she hasn't talked to you since my birthday and you haven't returned her calls, only texted saying you're busy. You're lucky I volunteered to come here, or she and Dad would be at your door now. You wouldn't want that because the way you look right now, Mom would be trying to get you in a bathtub so she could bathe you like when we were kids."

Without looking away from the television, I mumble, "I haven't felt like talking."

"Apparently, you haven't felt like showering or shaving either," he says sarcastically as he takes a seat on the couch next to me. I can feel his gaze burning against my face, waiting for me to say more, but when I say nothing, Parker continues, "What the hell is up with you, Drew? You were off at my party last week, and the silent treatment tells me something is going on. So, what is it?"

I take my eyes away from the television as the commentator yells, "Goal!" and set my attention on my brother as he stands a couple of feet from me with his hands on his hips. What do I say? We tell one another everything, but this is the one thing I've never discussed with anyone. Not even Parker.

I say the first thing that pops into my head. "I'm screwed up."

"No shit, Sherlock, but you're also stupid if you think I'm going to leave this alone because you tell me you're screwed up," he informs me, his eyes never leaving my face.

"I broke my rule. I fucking broke the one rule I've set for myself and kept for the last ten years," I confess, running my hands over my face. "I got too fucking cocky, Parks."

He sighs, walking over to the couch and taking a seat next to me, resting his elbows on his knees. Although we never discuss it, he knows what rule I'm talking about. A few minutes pass before either of us says anything.

"Dude, you started dating someone?" Parker sounds so shocked it almost makes me laugh.

"Nope. Not exactly, anyway," I respond, a little shock seeping into my own voice. "It's worse. Or better…no, it definitely feels worse right now."

As he looks over at me, I see the shock is now covering his entire face.

"Don't look at me like that," I tell him.

"Like what?" He tries to school his features.

"Like I told you, I have a twenty-inch penis," I joke. He cracks a smile and so do I for the first time in a while. There's something about being around Parker that makes it impossible for me to stay in a complete funk.

"Seriously, Drew, quit talking in riddles and get to the fucking point," Parker says, turning to face me.

"Her name is Rosie. We met by accident and became friends. She was different and funny and beautiful...and she had no idea. She has no idea," I tell him.

"And? This is a problem because?" he asks.

"The problem is I got cocky...I let my guard down. She came to me with a proposition because she wanted my help being more confident and dateable, so to speak. She wanted to be different. I tried to change her mind, and then she said she would just find someone else. I didn't like that at all. I didn't want her to get hurt by some douchebag. She convinced me she'd be fine and said she understood my rule. I made sure we knew there was a line I would never cross."

"So what? She didn't really understand? She fucking fell in love with you and tried crossing that line, didn't she?" Parker guesses, shaking his head at me.

"No," I confess. "I'm the one who fucking crossed the line."

You know in movies or cartoons where someone says something so shocking to another person that their mouths fall open? Parker just did it. He's staring at me, mouth open wide with disbelief.

"Close your mouth, Parker." I begin pacing when he shuts his mouth but remains silent, so I continue, "I wasn't as in control as I thought." The commentator yells, "Goal!" again, but I'm not interested in what's happening behind me. It was just a distraction today, so I reach for the remote I laid on the coffee table and switch the television off. "I crossed the line, and when I had my chance to prove to her I just might be capable of the commitment I told her I would never make, I blew it by running scared and showing my ass."

Parker looks like he wants to say something, but isn't sure what it should be.

"I pushed her away, and now she is scared to trust me. I hurt her. I became the douchebag I wanted to save her from when she approached me with this deal," I explain further.

"Does she want more with you?" he asks me, suddenly breaking his silence.

"I think so. Or at least I thought so…before…maybe," I stutter out. The idea she doesn't want more between us makes me nervous.

"What about you? Are you sure of what you want?" Parker continues shooting out questions, digging deeper, but I'm not sure where he's going.

"Yes. No…yes, it scares me. Parks, I miss her. No, I don't just miss Rosie. I ache for her. I physically feel her absence from my life," I confess shamelessly. "Jesus, Parker. How did I let myself get in this position?"

He stands and walks over to me, slapping his hand on top of my shoulder. "Damn, dude. I don't know, but you better think of something quick to fix it because I'm not dealing with your heartbroken ass for another ten years. Plus, Mom wouldn't be able to take it again."

Parker is right. I need to figure this out because I can't go on floating in this sea forever, or eventually, I'm going to drown.

Sitting on my board with my spandex-clad legs dangling in the frigid water, I wait for the perfect wave. I wait for the adrenaline rush that comes with it. The one that makes me feel free and excited when I allow it to take over. There's danger, a risk with every wave I take, especially the big ones because the reality is, we aren't in control out here. The ocean is. Mother Nature and all her unpredictable ways. I enjoy the risk and take it anyway.

It's the exact feeling I have when I see Rosie. Touch Rosie. Talk to Rosie. I'm not blind to the fact I didn't choose to take this risk because my heart was at stake. Now, I'm stuck trying to figure out how I can paddle back out and get my second chance.

My hair is still wet with salt water when I walk into The Roasting Company. I breathe in the scent of coffee beans that fills the air. Feeling relaxed and determined, I allow my eyes to roam over every face in the room, hoping to see one in particular.

"She hasn't been in the shop for over a week," a familiar English accent says from behind me.

Swinging around, I try to hide my disappointment from my features. "Who?" I ask, trying to act nonchalant. Andy's face doesn't change. He doesn't say anything; he only studies my face. I realize how idiotic I must sound. Who am I kidding? Not Andy. "All week?" I finally say.

"Sorry to disappoint you, mate," Andy consoles, squeezing my shoulder as he walks around me and heads for his position behind the counter. I want to tell him I'm not disappointed, but that would be a lie. I am disappointed, and I need to stop hiding how I feel when it comes to Rosie, or I'll never convince her I believe we belong to one another.

Instead, I turn to the counter to order, feeling a little resigned to the fact I need a better plan than finding her in the coffee shop or showing up on her doorstep. When I meet Andy's eyes, I shrug. "I need to talk to her." Telling him this small fact feels like I'm confessing my deepest secret, and that alone tells me it's a good thing Rosie isn't here. If she were, I would likely make our situation a bigger mess than it already is.

"Yes, mate. You do." He hands me my iced black coffee before continuing, "And she needs to talk to you. Do you want to chat a bit? I'm taking my break now."

I give him a nod then turn and head toward a table in the corner.

As I take a seat, I think about Andy's straightforward reply. He never sugarcoats anything; he just keeps it real. Always telling me as it is. It's what I like about him.

I'm deep in thought when he sits across from me a few minutes later and asks, "So tell me, mate. How are you going to fix this?" Okay. Right to the point. I look up at him and can't help the tiny smile that forms on my lips.

"Well, I have no damn clue, man. I've barely come to terms with my emotions myself; how can I convince her I'm someone she should bet on? Give her heart to me instead of running the other way," I answer honestly.

"I can't answer that for you. Only you and Rosie will know what it will take. You're the only two people who know what has transpired between the two of you. My only advice to you is this, Drew. Life can move swiftly by us. We often waste too much time forgetting to live it. Time is the one thing we act like we have so much of when in reality it's the one thing that's limited. So I can only tell you this about your situation: If you don't want to wake up one day and find that Rosie isn't waiting, then you need to be honest and reach out, take hold of her and savor every moment like it's your last," he offers.

His words hit me right in the chest. I heard every word he just said; I only wonder if I'm capable of doing what it takes. I wonder if I can allow myself to be vulnerable. To take the risk I've taken before.

Without another word, he stands and walks away, going back to work.

I've got a lot to figure out. If I want to convince Rosie I'm all in, it's going to take more than just saying it. I'm going to need something more. Be more.

CHAPTER Three

"**D**rew?" I hear a feminine voice say from behind me. My hand pauses on the door handle of The Roasting Company's entrance. Turning, I find the face of Sami smiling brightly at me.

Ah, Sami. One night on the beach of an impromptu bonfire party Parker decided to have after a day of surfing. Sand in all the wrong places, but fun and feisty nonetheless. I haven't seen her since, but I would like to pat myself on the back for remembering her name.

"Wow, Sami. It's been a while," I say, returning her smile. "How have you been?"

She takes a step closer, and her eyes get that familiar look in them anytime I run into a girl I shared some fun with and remember her name.

"I've been great. How about you?" she replies, face still bright.

"Good…great, I'll be even better once I get some caffeine in me." I gesture over my shoulder toward the coffee shop.

"I was headed in there for some coffee myself. Would you like to sit down and catch up for a bit?" she asks, a hopeful gleam in her eyes. Although I'm used to seeing this kind of look and am a pro at deflecting it, I realize Sami is harmless. It won't hurt to sit with her for a minute.

"Sure, I have a few minutes to catch up," I tell her, pulling the door open and holding it for her.

When we walk in, I notice the usual Saturday afternoon crowd, although the line is short. We each order and pay for our drinks, then we take a seat at an empty table in the middle of the room. Laughter and conversation around us, and Sami leans forward and takes a sip from her cup. I watch her, thinking about the fact that she's pretty. I never noticed. Well, okay, so I obviously noticed the night of the bonfire, but I didn't look at her beyond having a little fun in the sand with her. I feel a wave of shame move over me.

Before I know what I'm doing, I say, "I'm sorry I never called you."

She looks up me, a slightly startled look crossing her features. I can tell she isn't sure how to react to what I just said. Then, suddenly, a wide smile envelops her face. "Drew, I didn't expect you to call. You were very clear about what you did and didn't want. I was very aware of what I was doing. We had fun, and that's what we were both looking for that night."

It's true I'm always up front with anyone I've spent time with or been with when it comes to my intentions. But does it make it okay? I feel like I'm better than that, and they are too. I never even tried. So that begs the question, why did I break my rules when it came to Rosie?

"I still should've at least called or something," I repeat.

"Thank you. How's Parker?" she asks, moving on from that topic.

"He's good. You know Parker, he only cares about surfing, and that's what he does," I reply, thinking about my brother and the way he just does what he wants without apology.

She laughs, another smile lighting her face. "I do. I doubt that boy cares about anything else. No offense, but that's so typical for guys around here. Surfing is life."

Chuckling, I nod my head. "You know it. At least until we have something else to care about in our lives." Again, an ache makes itself known in the middle of my chest. God damn it. I gotta get out of here and figure this thing out with Rosie.

"Well, I better get going," I say, standing at the same time she does. "Yeah, me too," she concurs. "It was really great seeing you again, Drew. Maybe I'll see you around again sometime soon." Reaching out, she touches my arm lightly. I look down briefly at her hand resting on my arm, and then I lean forward and give her a hug. It's something I wouldn't normally do, but I'm trying to do things a little differently these days. As we pull back, Sami pecks me on the cheek. She gives me one last bright smile and leaves.

It's strange to think, but it's like the last fifteen minutes with Sami gave me the last dose of clarity I needed with regards to Rosie. I just need to get my plan together and then find Rosie.

Picking up my coffee from the table, I turn to the door and freeze.

Standing in a line that extends nearly to the door is Rosie. She's staring right at me, and from the look on her face, she saw me with Sami. I can't seem to move, and she isn't blinking. We're just staring. Doing nothing. She breaks contact first, when the guy standing behind her leans over her shoulder and whispers in her ear. When he straightens, I see his face and recognize him as Travis. The same guy she went out with on the night of our big fight. Instantly, I feel sick. It must be written on my face because her expression changes too.

Quickly as I can move, I make my way to the door. Just as I reach it, I take one last glance behind me, and I find Rosie is still watching me. Except this time she isn't the only one. Travis is watching me too, and judging by the look on his face, he isn't excited to see me.

I need to get out of here.

Turning back around, I push my way out onto the street, away from Rosie, the one girl I've wanted more than for just one night.

By the time I reach my apartment, I'm even more confused about how I'm feeling.

Misunderstandings.

Miscommunications.

Guilt.

Heartache.

Fear.

I allowed this to happen. Can I really be angry? If she cares so much about me, then why is she out with him? As soon as I think this, I try to recall if Rosie has ever told me exactly how she feels, or did I just make it all up in my head based on what I'm feeling?

Slowly, I climb the stairs of the front stoop to my building, trying to work through all of these emotions. Why did I run out of there? Why am I always running away from what I want? I want Rosie. I'm going back. Whipping around, I come to a dead stop when I see her standing at the bottom of the steps. She's turned partially away as if she came, but decided to turn away before letting me know she was here.

"Don't leave..." I say almost desperately. "Rosie."

She pauses, but doesn't turn around. I know I need to think of something. I know I need to touch her. Moving toward her, I reach out, lightly gripping her wrist. She turns her head toward me, eyes wide and full of something I'm not quite sure I can put my finger on. Rosie simply shrugs her shoulders. It's like she doesn't know what to say either.

"Do you want to come up?" I ask, although I'm afraid of her answer. She nods, and we walk up the steps together. I don't let her go until we get inside as if my hand on her wrist was keeping her from leaving me.

We remain silent as we walk up the two flights to my loft, even as I unlock the door and push it open. Neither Rosie nor I says a word when I gesture for her to go in ahead of me, or when I close the door behind us. I watch her walk deeper into the light, airy one-room apartment. It's about nine hundred square feet of open space. The colors are masculine, light gray and blue hues. The area I deem my bedroom is separated from the rest of the room by a large, wide-cubed bookshelf, filled with all of my favorite books and framed photos of my family and me. In all the months Rosie and I slept together, she never once stepped foot into my apartment. I always met her downstairs, but never brought her up. We always spent time in her apartment.

Having her here feels right. Her eyes roam over every inch of the room; I regard her expression as she does this, noticing the way she pauses to gaze at certain things. I feel vulnerable because this isn't just the first time Rosie has been here, but it's the first time any woman has been here. She's seeing a private side of me that only my family or close friends know.

My eyes never leave her face as I try to determine if I can let myself trust her. She was on a date. A date. And although I know I have no right to be upset by this, I am. I've been missing her, and she was on a date.

"You were on a date. With him," I announce, my voice more accusing than I intended, but unable to help myself.

She turns to face me, a sardonic smile on her face. "Are you serious?" Her hands go to her hips.

Between the bitter look on her face and the disconcerted tone to her question, I feel myself go on the defensive. I know it's irrational.

Taking a step toward her, my voice raises a little. "Yes, I'm serious. You were on a date with that Travis guy."

Her face turns a pretty shade of red as she steps toward me. We're almost toe to toe. "And...and you were on a date with that girl!" I've never heard Rosie raise her voice, but I can see her hands are shaking.

"I wasn't," I retort. "I ran into her, and we sat down for no more than fifteen minutes catching up. She's friends with my brother. But you were! You were on a date."

"You weren't on a date?" she says, a little less force behind her words.

"No. I wasn't," I repeat.

"I was. Sort of," she says. "He called and asked me to coffee. It was harmless. I..."

I inch a little closer to her. "Rosie?" I say her name like a question. It's barely a whisper from my lips. Her eyes gleam with a hint of moisture. I feel guilty all over again.

"I saw you...and that girl. I couldn't think, and I just left him. I left him and ran after you. I can't think clearly anymore, Drew." I'm standing so close to her now that she has no choice but to look up at me.

"I miss you, Rosie, and it kills me to see you with someone else," I confess. My hand goes up and cups her face. She closes her eyes and leans into my palm. Her skin is soft and cool to the touch. "I know I have no right, but I miss you."

Pivotal moment number two...

*P*ivotal moment number two happened at the most unexpected time. Maybe I wasn't prepared for it because I've never had one. A morning after. I almost didn't leave. Part of me didn't want to leave her lying there. Alone. But I did leave. The morning after...

My eyes flash open, and I find myself staring up at an unfamiliar clock on the wall.

Rosie.

It's six thirty in the morning. I stayed all night. I know I agreed to stay, but that was before...

My heart races at the thought. I never stay. I resist the urge to jump out of bed because I know Rosie is asleep next to me. I can feel her curled up at my back. I can feel her warmth against my skin. Her scent and the smell of sex linger in the air around us.

For a moment, I want nothing more than to stay here next to her in all the places I touched her only hours ago. But I can't. I'm not that guy. I shouldn't be here still. Slowly, I lift myself out of bed, then quickly gather my clothes, putting them on quietly so *not to wake her, and heading for the door.*

When I touch the doorknob, I stop.

Motionless.

I take six deep breaths, fighting against these unwanted feelings Rosie has stirred within me. I know I'm an asshole for leaving like this, but she knew. She knows. I told her. It was part of our agreement.

No strings.

No commitment.

No sleepovers.

Just sex. This is the deal she made. The problem is I can't seem to walk away.

Before I know what I'm doing, I turn back to where I left Rosie sleeping soundly. As I quietly approach her, I see the soft rise and fall of her chest. It sends a chill over my skin. Unable to resist the need, I reach out and lightly brush the hair from her face. She's beautiful. I'm so damn scared of screwing up and hurting her.

Again, the uneasy feeling I had before fills my chest until I'm nearly gasping for breath. I take three quick steps back. I turn and leave without another glance.

This.

Was.

The.

Deal.

CHAPTER *Four*

Opening her eyes, she looks into mine. "I've missed you, too."

Those words, her sweet scent, and her soft skin are all it takes me to forget everything else I had planned for when I had her standing before me again. All thoughts other than touching her, kissing her, leave my mind.

Sliding my hand from her cheek and into her hair, I tug gently, tilting her face up to align with mine before my lips crash against hers. She tastes just as I remember. It's everything I've longed for over the last few weeks.

Rosie doesn't resist me; she opens to me, and I pull her closer, deepening our kiss.

Her hands move around my waist and under my shirt, clawing their way up my back. She holds on to me so tightly, it's impossible for us to get any closer. I pull my mouth away from hers and search her eyes for any sign she doesn't want this too. There isn't anything there other than pure desire. Joy surges through me, and I can't help the smile that spreads across my face. Then it's gone because I only want to touch her, and it seems she only can think of touching me. Our movements become more frantic, each of us pulling at the other's clothes until every piece is lying on the floor.

We're kissing again, my mouth devouring hers, making up for

every day I haven't kissed her.

Rosie wraps her legs around me as I lift her by the waist and walk us around the bookcase to my bed, never breaking our kiss. My hands cup her round, tight ass as she plunges her tongue deeper into my mouth. Her eyes open and look into mine. Normally, I'd feel uncomfortable with the way she's watching me, but instead, I savor the familiarity of the trust I see there. It's something I thought I had completely lost.

When we reach the edge of the bed, I set Rosie on her feet.

Her eyes trail down my body. Taking her time, she moves her fingertips along every plain, every muscle of my torso until she reaches my thighs. A chill runs over my skin, her touch is enough to bring me to my knees. She's just about to take me into her hands, but I stop her.

"My turn," I whisper. "I won't be using my hands, though."

Leaning forward, I press my lips to the soft skin of her collarbone and slowly pepper kisses across her skin, between the cleft of her perfect breast, to the opposite shoulder, then continue my way down. When I reach the flat area of her stomach around her belly button, Rosie releases a low moan, letting me know it's affecting her just as much as it is me to have my lips on her. I don't stop, placing my lips on the inside of both of her inner thighs, my tongue leaving a trail to her most sensitive area. Just before I reach her core, I hear her release another soft sigh, full of anticipation. My mouth invades her wetness, her thighs clenching around my head as I push my tongue deeper. She tastes so good; I have a hard time staying still from the throbbing hardness between my legs. Satisfying her brings me so close to the edge, I nearly explode. When she starts screaming my name and pulling me close, I almost can't take it. Then she gasps my name one more time.

I place one last kiss there before standing up; her eyes are closed.

"Open your eyes, Rosie," I demand gently. She acquiesces my request. Her eyes shine with a want that mirrors my own. "I've missed you." I know I've already told her this more than once, but I've never told a woman this before. And I haven't felt this way in ten years. It means something.

Dipping my head, I kiss her—a gentle, deliberate touch of my lip—before taking it deeper as I lay her back onto the bed and move over her.

When I look down into her eyes, she's gazing back at me. "Drew, I've missed you too," she tells me, her voice quiet. Timid. Maybe even a little scared, but I'm going to show her what she means to me and hopefully take that fear away.

Turning to my nightstand, I pull the drawer open, taking out a condom. As I put it on, I glance over at her lying on the bed. She's peering at me beneath her lashes, her breathing becoming more erratic as I roll the condom down my shaft. When I'm hovering over her once more, our mouths are pulled together again by some magnetic force between us. I can't get enough of her, and I know she's ready for me.

As I position myself between her legs, I wait until she opens her eyes. She looks up, putting her hands on my ass, suddenly pulling me forward at the same time I push into her. We both gasp the other's name at the connection, a desperation to be as close to one another as possible. Once we're fully connected, we pause, panting with need but unwilling to move, savoring this moment when we're one.

When it's impossible to wait any longer, we both begin to move, her tightness clenching around me, building the pleasure with each movement. I try to take everything she has to offer and give her the same in return. I'm panting her name over and over until I'm unsure I'm still speaking out loud.

Without pulling out of her, I roll us over until Rosie is positioned above me.

Giving her control, Rosie never misses a beat. She moves slowly at first then faster until we're both coming apart and she's falling against my chest. My name leaves her lips in an almost incoherent sigh against my chest.

After a few minutes, and once our breathing returns to normal, Rosie moves off of me and to my side. I reach the side of the bed, discarding the condom in the wastebasket next to my nightstand.

Rolling back over, I notice Rosie hasn't moved, so I put an arm around her and pull her against me. I place a kiss on the side of her head. "Rosie, I know I keep saying it, but I mean it…I missed you so much," I tell her again.

She pulls my hand from her midsection up to her mouth and places a kiss on my palm. "Me too, Drew," she reveals again. "So much. But I'm still scared."

God, I don't want her to be afraid of us. Of me. Can't she see it? Feel it?

Instead of saying anything, I place another kiss to her temple and pull her tighter against my chest. I don't know how long it is before we're both sound asleep.

Without opening my eyes, I inhale deeply, smelling the aftermath of our lovemaking. It surrounds me, and I feel the excitement moving through me all over again. A wide, toothy grin spreads across my face as I reach over to pull Rosie over to me.

I come up empty. I quickly sit up in bed, looking around.

I'm scanning the single open room of my loft. The only room I haven't checked is the bathroom, but I know without looking she's gone. Rosie left. I left her once. Is this what it felt like? It's like someone punched me in the gut, knocking the breath from me. Walking to the window, I look out, catching a glimpse of the few early risers on the streets through the light, foggy morning.

I feel sick. Not only because of the ache in my heart, but also over the idea I have done this to Rosie. More than once. I hurt her and now I'm hurting. I'm going to have to live with it, just as she did. But, before I do that, I'm going to need a minute.

One minute. Damn. One minute won't be enough, but it will have to do. For now.

I place my hand against the cool glass and try pushing the hurt I feel out. Forty-five seconds to remember I made this bed so I have to lie in it. I said no strings. Thirty seconds to accept the fact I pushed her away. To understand I'm the reason she is scared. Is hurting still. Fifteen seconds to recognize that I'm the only one who can fix this mess I put us in. It's not up to Rosie or anyone else to fix it. Just me. Five seconds to wallow in the fact for one night I thought maybe she'd accepted I care about her, and we could move forward. To accept it isn't and shouldn't be that easy for the two of us to move forward. It will take more than a few "I missed yous" and incredible sex for her to know without a doubt I'm hers. It's going to take a whole hell of a lot more. With no acceptance seconds left, I back away from the window, wipe my eyes, and head for the shower.

I'm not the Drew I thought I wanted to be. I'm not capable of letting Rosie slip away from me. She deserves more. I deserve more.

Although there's no one to hear me, my voice echoes through the room when I say, "I'm not that Drew anymore. I'll prove it."

CHAPTER *Five*

Walking up to the front door, there's only one person I want to speak to right now. When I called earlier, Dad said he'd be leaving, but Mom would be home.

When I reach the door, I raise my hand to knock, but the door swings open before I even touch it.

"Andrew, honey. What's going on?" My mom doesn't even wait for me to get in the house. She just cuts right to the chase. She has always had a way of knowing when something is bothering one of us. It's the reason I've avoided her and my dad for the most part since Parker's birthday party.

She has perspective. A keen ability to stand on the outside of the situation and guide you to make the decision you're meant to make. All without insinuating her feelings on the matter—it's her specialty.

I lean in to hug her, and she pulls me tight against her. It's been a while since I let her hold me like this, reminiscent of when I was a kid. "Mom. How are you?" I say, my voice muffled against her.

Pulling back, she looks at me like I'm insane and slaps me on the shoulder as she closes the door behind us. "Andrew Nallen, you did not come here to talk about me, so let's quit avoiding what you obviously need to talk about with me." Right to the point as usual.

She leads me into the kitchen, setting a coffee cup on the bar, in front of one of the stools. I take a seat when she turns, pouring coffee into my cup, then into the one she pulled out for herself.

"So what's happening, honey? Parker didn't want to say anything when I questioned him, although he led me to believe it has something to do with a girl." She takes a sip of coffee then continues, "I worry about you."

"Mom, you can stop worrying. It's nothing that bad, I just..." I tell her, but then she interrupts.

"Don't tell me to stop worrying. I'm your mother, and I'll always worry. You just never been the same since La—"

This time, I interrupt her. "Don't. This situation with Rosie has nothing to do with her." I can't even say her name. A rush of memories fills my mind.

"I'm Laura," she introduces herself. Her voice is nice, soft.

"I'm Drew," I respond. I look her over. She's pretty. Sweet. I've been talking to her for the last five minutes, and we're only just now getting around to introducing ourselves, the crowd of the party around us. It's the first party I've attended so far during my sophomore year at UCSC. I've been trying to stay focused on my grades.

Laura smiles. It brightens her eyes. She reaches her hand out and runs it down my chest.

She's a little more forward than I'm comfortable with, but I'm a guy, and it does something to me when she smiles.

I see Parker making his way across the room toward me. He has that irritated look like someone pissed him off, so I think fast because I know he's going to be ready to leave.

"Well, Laura, my brother is headed this way and looks like he's ready to leave. So I'm going to ask you out. Do you want to go out with me sometime?" I ask her, Parker only five feet from me.

She grabs me and presses her mouth against mine in a quick, passionate kiss.

"Yeah, I think I'd like that, Drew," Laura replies, licking her bottom lip.

After we exchange numbers and I walk away, two voices are talk-

ing to me, one with a real brain warning me to be careful, and the other telling me to enjoy myself.

My mom lays her hand over mine. "Andrew, every action and decision you've made when it comes to your personal life since you were nineteen years old has had to do with Laura."

"Mom…" I start to disagree.

"No, Andrew. It's true. We've all watched you detach from the person we've always known. Of course, not toward us. We recognize in this aspect you've remained the same, but in your personal life and decisions, Andrew, you changed. It has been a struggle to mind my own business because you've always been the one out of all your brothers with the biggest capacity to love. Instead, I left you alone. We all left you alone, hoping one day you'd stop being a game boy."

"A game boy?" I question, laughter leaving me on the end of my question.

"Yeah, you know, Kelsea always calls you a game boy. A guy who won't commit to one girl and is a serial dater," she explains, taking another sip of her coffee.

A loud, boisterous laugh escapes me. I laugh so hard my insides hurt.

"I don't know why you're laughing; I didn't say it. Kelsea did, and it wasn't a compliment." She sounds a little offended I'm laughing at her.

Finally, I gain a little composure. "Mom, I love you. It's called a playboy. Kelsea calls me a playboy, not a game boy."

Waving me off, she dismisses her mistake, "Oh, well, whatever. Game boy…playboy, it doesn't matter. That isn't you."

Shaking my head, a small laugh slips out again. "Okay."

"Okay? You let Laura take away ten years from you. Why?" she asks me bluntly.

How do I answer this? Is that what I did? Did I let my past and Laura dictate the way I've lived my life for the last ten years? Yes, I guess I have let it take over. An ache forms in the middle of my chest.

Laura and I have gone out quite a bit over the last six months. She's nice and funny. Of course, easy on the eyes. But I feel like a dick because we slept together on the first date. And the second. And third. I stopped feeling so bad because as much as I was trying to avoid distractions from school, Laura is a distraction. I think I've fallen for her. Laura seems to think we were meant to meet that night. I think she might be right.

When I pull up to her dorm, she comes running out. I've been busy with exams the last few weeks, so I haven't seen very much of her. I have one last test tomorrow before winter break begins, but Laura begged me to meet her. I wanted to see her too because I think I want to tell her how I feel. She said she has something she needs to tell me.

I get out and open the car door for her. When she reaches me, I place a kiss on her soft lips; it feels nice.

"Hey," I greet her.

"Hey, I've missed you so much," she tells me, throwing her arms around my neck. I return her embrace. It's definitely time to tell her.

We pull apart, and I smile down at her before she gets in the car. I close the door and quickly walk around to my side of the car. When I get in, she immediately grabs my hand. Looking over at her, I feel conflicted and worried, but I'm not sure about what exactly.

"Uh, are you hungry?" I ask her, not sure what else to say.

"Yes, starving...can we go somewhere quiet? I need to talk to you. It's important," she practically begs, her tone strange.

"Sure...okay, I need to talk to you about something, too," I reply, pulling away from the curb and heading for one of the local cafés close to the school.

Once we get to the café and we're seated at a corner table, Laura begins acting stranger.

"Laura, are you okay?" I ask her, a little concerned.

"Yeah, yeah, I'm good," she says.

Reaching my hand across the table, I lay mine over hers.

"I wanted to tell you something. I'm just not sure how to say it," I begin, watching her. Her eyes go wide. She looks nervous. Like she's about to come out of her skin. I feel like I might come out of mine. I've

never felt this way about a girl. What if she doesn't feel the same? As Parker said, what if she does? "Laura, I think we—" I try to continue.

"Drew, I'm pregnant," she blurts out.

Did I hear her right? "You're...you're what?" I stutter.

"I'm pregnant. It's yours, of course." She's so matter-of-fact about it. How can she be so calm? I feel like I'm going to throw up.

"I'm nineteen. We just met. I'm not even close to finishing school yet. I don't have a job. We just met. I only just realized I might like you more than a little." I don't even know what I'm saying while I look at her, just talking. I know words are coming out of my mouth, but I don't know what.

"I know...but, maybe," she starts to say.

My eyes go wide. "How did this happen? We used protection," I say.

"I don't know, but...are you going to leave me?" she asks me, one lone tear slipping down her cheek.

Am I going to leave her? Oh, shit. No. I wouldn't. My parents wouldn't...my parents. Fuck.

"Drew?" she says in barely a whisper.

This time, when I look up, I realize my life just changed. I made choices that have consequences. I like her; maybe I love her. A baby. Shit, I was thinking I wanted to introduce Laura to my family. I wanted to see how this progressed between us. See if I can focus on her and school and life.

Reaching across the table again, I take Laura's hand into mine this time and give her a reassuring squeeze. "No, it's going to be okay. I'll take care of you. Of the baby. I'm all in. We'll do this together. I'm committed to you and the baby," I try to convince her. Maybe I'm try-ing to convince myself, scared out of my mind, but knowing this is the right thing.

"Drew?" my mom says, breaking me from my thoughts.

"Mom, I think I've screwed up this time," I admit to her. For the first time, I realize I've been building a wall for a long time, pretending to be content with how I was living my life.

"Why this time, Drew?" she asks me, understanding in her voice, but questioning me as I knew she would.

"Because I was an untrusting bastard. Because I pushed away a girl I actually have a connection with because I was scared. I've been a coward," I tell her. When I look over at her, I don't see sympathy, but I do see understanding.

"Andrew, you're not a coward. You were just careful. Maybe too careful, but definitely not a coward. No one blames you for what happened. You were so trusting and young at the time."

"Mom, I haven't really lived life for ten years because of one person's actions. It hasn't really mattered until now. Until Rosie. I hurt her because I let someone hurt me years before I ever met her," I say, feeling disgusted with myself. "I hurt myself."

"You have, and I've watched you because your father and I always vowed never to interfere in our children's lives." I hear the heartbreak in her voice and realize I've also been hurting my parents.

It has been two months since I hurt my parents when I told them I was going to be a dad. That I got Laura, a girl I barely know, pregnant. At first, they yelled, then they said they would stand behind me. And Laura.

They have honored their commitment. I've honored my commitment.

Pulling up to Laura's dorm, I park the car, full of excitement. I've missed every doctor appointment she has had so far. I was supposed to miss today because of my design class, but I'm skipping because this is important. I grab the stuffed bunny I bought for the baby, grinning at the ridiculous green overalls it's wearing.

Laura is going to be so excited because I know she was disappointed when I told her the appointment was at the same time as my class. I know things will feel even more real, especially because she hasn't started showing yet.

When I reach her door, I hear arguing, and before I knock, I hear my name.

"Laura, you're insane. Drew is going to get suspicious. How are

you going to pull this off?" a female voice I don't recognize says on the other side of the door.

"I don't know, but I will. I have to figure something out. I can't lose him," I hear Laura say.

"You're running out of time. How are you going to explain the timing?" the voice says.

What in the hell is going on? What will I be suspicious of? I hate eavesdropping, but I can't seem to make my presence known.

"I know...I just fell so hard for him and I...I just said it. I told him I was pregnant thinking I could get pregnant once I convinced him. I knew he was a good guy from the beginning and would do the right thing. I knew he would commit to me and this baby," Laura explained.

"Laura!" the girl exclaimed. "You aren't pregnant! Do you realize how crazy this is?"

"He was going to end things between us. I didn't know what else to do, so I blurted out the first thing that popped into my head," Laura tries reasoning further.

I feel the bile move up my throat. I'm going to be sick. Did I just hear her right? There's no baby?

There.

Is.

No.

Baby.

Shaking, I turn the knob and throw the door open, letting it bang against the wall.

Laura and her friend turn, facing me with shocked looks on their faces. Immediately, she tries to school her features of the worry she is surely feeling.

"Drew! What are you doing here?" her shaky voice says.

"Laura. Why?" I ask, the sick feeling only intensifying. "Laura. Why would you fucking do this?" I stalk toward her. "I committed to you. I made promises to you and let you flip my life and family upside down because of a lie. The saddest part is you lied because you thought I was going to break things off with you, but I wasn't. I was going to tell you I was falling for you. Now, I have fallen for you and it's been

based on a lie."

She reaches a hand toward me, tears slipping down her cheeks.

"A fucking lie!" I yell as I dodge her grasp. "Don't fucking touch me or come near me!"

"I love you!" she shouts, reaching for me again.

"This isn't love. You don't know love and neither do I. This is a lie!"

I turn to walk out the door, and I never look back.

That one moment changed me. The loss of trust. The loss of innocence. The loss of a baby. A life. A commitment that I already loved. It wasn't real. I only thought I loved it.

I blink back the tears that want to fall. "I'm sorry, Mom. I'm sorry I closed myself off to everyone. I'm sorry for hurting you. Dad. Myself. And I'm so damn sorry I hurt Rosie. I need to fix this. This is too important. This isn't a lie. This thing with Rosie is real," I acknowledge.

"Oh, Andrew, don't apologize. We love you no matter what, even if you are a game boy," she says, one corner of her mouth tipped up.

I laugh so hard because this time, she thinks she's funny. It's just like my family to use humor to tame a serious conversation.

"Do you love this girl?" she asks me, suddenly serious.

I look at her and say, "I think I might, but I do know I'm definitely falling."

"Then show her. Respect her. Do the opposite of whatever you've been doing and prove it. You need to be the one," my mother tells me. Little does she know, her words are perfect. And I know just what to do.

Let go of the past. Move forward. Prove to Rosie I want only her by listening to my mother and doing exactly what she just advised me to do.

CHAPTER Six

Determined, I knock three times hard on the door of Rosie's apartment and wait.

Shuffling from foot to foot, I try to replay in my head what I will say to her. The way I feel and the things I hope she will listen to before she pushes me away again. I feel like she wants the same things I want, but she's been hurt too by not only me but her ex-boyfriend. So she's weary of promises. Rosie will need action, and that's what I plan to give to her.

When the door opens, I start to say her name but stop short when I realize it isn't Rosie.

It's Abbey. She looks wary.

"Drew, Rosie isn't here right now," she tells me, a guarded tone hugging her words.

"Abbey, I know you don't trust me, but if Rosie is here, I need to talk to her, please," I beg.

I can see a look cross her face that tells me she hears the desperation in my voice.

"Drew, convince me. Tell me why you're here, because Rosie called me over for Ben and Jerry's and a '90s cult classic movie binge. She only does that when she needs to forget, or she's feeling conflicted. This is the second time we've done this in two months. The first time was because of you, and I suspect this time is because of you, too. Although I don't know because she isn't back from the store with our Chunky Monkey, so spill it. Tell me why I should let you in here." Abbey's little speech is full of warning. She knows I've hurt Rosie and she isn't going to let it happen again.

"I didn't mean to hurt her. I know I did, but I hurt myself too," I tell her. Abbey places her hand on her hip. She needs more convincing. "Please, Abbey. I need to fix this between us. I walk away from her, and I can't let her walk away from me. I'm falling in love with her, and I need to prove I want more than just a no-strings relationship with her. I just need the chance to do it," I continue to pour my heart out and beg. Maybe if I convince Abbey, there's a chance I can convince Rosie, too.

Abbey doesn't say a word; she just opens the door wider to allow me through.

I pause for only second, then walk past her without a word. When she closes the door, Abbey walks over to the table and picks up her purse, slinging it over her shoulder.

"You're leaving?" I ask her, genuinely confused. I was willing to tell Rosie how I feel regardless of Abbey's presence.

"Yes, you convinced me. It wasn't necessarily your words, you kind of need to work on that part, but it was the look in your eyes. I'm trusting you to do right by my girl," she answers me honestly.

"Thank you," I express.

"No need to thank me, just don't hurt her or I'll hurt you," she threatens.

I nod, watching her turn and walk toward the door without another word. I feel confident this might work. For some reason, Abbey's approval gives me hope.

She pauses in the doorway, and without turning around, she says, "Oh, and enjoy my Chunky Monkey. Just a tip, let Rosie have all of your bites with banana in it. It might help the cause." Then she closes the door without another word.

I smile because again, I think I just might have a chance after all.

I'm standing in the middle of her living room when she walks through the door. She isn't looking up but instead digging through the bag, searching for something.

"Don't be mad, Abbey, but I think the bag boy forgot to put the Junior Mints in the bag," she apologizes.

"Abbey didn't tell me there would be Junior Mints, too," I proclaim before Rosie even has a chance to see me.

A loud yelp slips between her lips and she stumbles forward, dropping the bag in the process.

I rush forward, bending down to pick up the bag she just dropped. "I'm sorry, I didn't mean to startle you," I apologize, looking up her at shocked expression.

"Drew, you're here!" she says, sounding surprised.

Standing, I walk over and place the bag of groceries on the kitchen counter. Turning, I see Rosie still in the same spot, watching me with trepidation.

"I am. I came to see you, and Abbey let me in. I hope you aren't mad at her; she resisted at first," I explain.

"Uh, no. I mean, why?" she stutters.

"Because you left," I tell her. A look of guilt passes over her face before it turns into a sort of resolve…a sadness.

"You don't do mornings after, Drew. I was at your place, so I had to be the one to leave," she reminds me, as if I need reminding.

"You didn't have to leave. In fact, I didn't want you to leave. I—"

I'm still talking when she interrupts me. "We shouldn't have slept together!"

I step toward her; we're close, and I can smell her soft, floral perfume. "Don't say that. Don't even think it," I demand in a low voice. Reaching out, I cup her soft cheek gently. "Please don't say that again. We both know that isn't true.

I can see her bottom lip trembling; tears glisten at the edges of her eyelids.

"Rosie, I know you're scared. I know it's my fault, but please just hear me out. Then, if you still want me to leave…" I swallow then continue, "I'll leave."

She turns until her back is to me. My hand falls to my side; I don't even try to stop her. Rosie walks to the couch and sits down, her eyes focused on her hands in her lap.

"Talk," she states quietly. "I'll listen to what you have to say."

I walk over to the couch, kneeling in front of her and taking her hands in mine.

"I know I tried telling you before what I was beginning to feel, or rather what I felt. Every word was true. I just expressed myself wrong. I was a fool to say I *thought* when I *knew*. I knew that night what I felt. I tried telling you but was too stupid and too afraid to feel. I want to try with you, strings and all." I pour my heart out and lay it out there in between us. I never take my eyes off her face, although she's been looking down the whole time. When the last word leaves my mouth, her attention is fully on me.

"What are you saying?" she questions.

"I'm saying I've been an idiot. I'm saying I want to see if what I think we have between us is real." I smile. "And I believe it is. I'm saying I want to date you."

Standing, I pull her with me by her hands, and she comes willingly.

"Date me…I…" she stutters out.

"Yes, but I have one stipulation. Or shall we say rule?" I propose.

A tiny smile forms on her lips and a flicker of amusement lights her eyes. "Oh, really?

"Yep. We're only allowed to date one another, no one else," I insist then continue. "No one else at all. Only dates. No sex. I need you to teach me…because you know things. You know things like how to be in a monogamous relationship."

She throws her head back in a loud, boisterous laugh. "Oh, really, and you want me to teach you?" she teases back.

"Can you just say yes or no, Rosie? If it's no, I have no one waiting in the wings, and I'll be forced to stalk you for eternity, so please say yes," I tease her.

Her face falls. "Drew, why are you doing this?"

"I told you, I care about you. I think we have something, and I realized I couldn't just tell you how I feel, I needed to show you. I want you to believe me when I tell you that I want only you." I'm practically begging now.

This time, it's Rosie who places her hand along my jawline and looks me directly in the eyes.

"Yes," she whispers.

"Are you sure?" I ask her, suddenly worried.

"Yes," she reaffirms then rises slowly on her tiptoes and places her lips against mine.

My arms instantly wrap around her, pulling her closer, deepening the kiss. Kissing Rosie. It's something I never want to stop doing, but as we both begin to run our hands over the other's body, I recognize I need to stop. I just promised her a dating-only arrangement, and I'm not letting either one of us break it. I'm going to make sure this works, so I push away from her.

"We need to stop," I utter with little conviction.

"We do?" Rosie says this like a question. "We do," she repeats, but more as a statement this time.

"We do," I reiterate.

"Ben and Jerry!" Rosie exclaims, startling me. She dashes around me and into the kitchen.

When I turn around, her bottom lip is puckered out, and she's holding two pints of ice cream. From the look on her face, I have a feeling the Chunky Monkey is a little milky. A chuckle slips out as I walk toward her, watching her face.

"Don't you dare laugh!" she scolds me. "I love Ben and Jerry."

When I reach her, I take the Chunky Monkey from her hands and turn to stick them in the freezer.

"Are you trying to make me jealous?" I tease, pecking her on the end of her nose in the process. "You're damn cute, Rosie Fisher," I compliment.

She laughs. "I didn't know the infamous Drew Nallen got jealous."

"I do when it comes to you," I respond seriously.

Something flickers in the depths of her eyes, then a soft smile forms on her face. "I think we need another rule," she says, a new desire shining in her eyes.

"Oh, we do?" I question. Rosie takes me by the hand and begins leading me out of the kitchen area and to the...door? "Wait, did I say something wrong?"

When we reach the door, she pulls it open and pushes me gently through the threshold.

"Rosie?" I look at her desperately.

"For this new arrangement to work, we need this last rule," she begins, a humorous expression on her face, yet she looks like this rule isn't something she necessarily wants. "The last rule is we must only see one another in public places until we know where this is going because frankly, Drew, it's the only way I'm keeping my hands off of you," she confesses.

Before I know what's happening, Rosie leans forward, giving me one last hard and passionate kiss. Pulling back, she quickly says, "I can't wait to see you again," then she closes the door in my face.

A surprised laugh booms out of me as I turn and walk away. She is so damn adorable and smooth as hell. When I am a few feet away from her door, I turn and jog back. I get as close as I can, and shout, "I accept these rules, Rosie Fisher, and I can't wait to see you again, too."

CHAPTER *Seven*

"Y ou're the biggest dumbass on the planet," Tyler tells Jasper when he spills his coffee on his shirt.

Taking a drink of my coffee, I debate in my head whether I should inform Tyler that's the pot calling the kettle black, but before I can say anything, Parker says it for me. "Tyler, you're also the biggest dumbass on the planet, so I'd keep your comments to yourself."

I start laughing so hard I almost spit my coffee across the table.

"What are you laughing at, douchebag?" Tyler asks, sounding annoyed.

Once again Parker takes the opportunity to give Tyler a dose of what he dishes when he slaps him upside the head.

This is typical Nallen brother banter when we're around one another. We give one another shit, but someone else tries to come at one of us, and they have the whole family to deal with. When we throw Kelsea, our only sister, in the mix, forget about it. She can hold her own with us. We drive our mom crazy, and my dad only adds fuel to the fire. Our family dynamic is interesting, to say the least.

Putting my hands between my brothers, I say, "Dudes, knock it off! We're in public."

Jasper starts laughing then the rest of us join in. I punch him in the shoulder, and he rubs it while he says, "It's been too long since we've done this."

"Gah, you sound like such a pansy-ass sometimes," I jab at him.

I wait for Jasper's response, but it doesn't come. In fact, they're all suddenly unusually quiet.

"What the hell is—" I start to ask them, but I'm interrupted before I can finish my question.

"Hello...hi...uh...hey," I hear from behind me. I'd recognize that voice anywhere and when I turn around in my chair, I realize the exact reason why they're all struck speechless.

Rosie is standing behind me, her elbow awkwardly bent, her hand in the air in a sort of shy wave hello. She's dressed in a tight, low-cut burgundy sweater with a pencil skirt that hugs all of her curves, and a pair of knee-high boots. You can see all of her, and she's fully covered. I love it and hate it at the same time. This is a prime example of what I always knew, and she never understood: she's beautiful and noticeable without even trying.

I stand quickly, wanting to shield her from my brothers' gawking gazes, but realize it's a ridiculous thought. "Hey!" It's the only thing I can seem to get out.

"Hey," she repeats with a smile that lights up my whole world.

"I was going to call you later to see if you wanted to have dinner tonight," I tell her. "I guess now I don't need to call. Is it too short notice?" I ramble, feeling nervous. This is new for me; I can't remember the last time someone actually made me nervous.

"Oh, no...no, not at all. I would love to have dinner tonight," she beams. "I'll let you get back to your friends. I didn't mean to interrupt."

Before I can tell Rosie she isn't interrupting, a hand appears between us. It takes hold of hers, bringing it up to his lips. Tyler.

"Hi, I don't think we've met. I'm Tyler, Drew's younger and very available brother," he flirts.

Suddenly, Parker appears next to me. "Tyler, don't be an asshole," he says before turning to Rosie. "You must be Rosie. Drew told me all about you." He gives her his mega-watt smile that usually flips girls so fast they don't know what hit them. "Please forgive Tyler, we only let him out of the house everyone once in a while, so his manners leave something to be desired," Parker continued.

I expect Jasper to pop his head in, but for once he's smart and stays seated.

I pull Rosie's hand from Tyler's and lead her to the table. "Do you have time to sit for a bit?"

Eyes wide, Rosie nods her head. "Yeah, sure."

She must notice Jasper sitting at the table, drinking his coffee, pretending not to care about the beautiful girl sitting next to him, because she turns to him. "Hi, I'm Rosie," she says sweetly. I scoot closer to her as Tyler and Parker sit back down.

"Hey, I'm Jasper. It's nice to meet you. So, you're Drew's... uh... friend?" he inquires.

"We're dating," I chime in before Rosie can answer. Her head whips around and her face shows me she's happily surprised by my response.

I don't have to look at my brother's faces to know each of them is staring at me in shock.

"Uh...uh... well, that's great," Jasper says, still looking confused but trying to hide it.

"Oh man, I need to find out what you did to get my brother to use the 'd' word," Tyler jibes.

Rosie's eyes are bouncing around the table, an overwhelmed look on her face.

"Okay...okay, let's give her a break. Poor thing hasn't been able to say a word because we've been in her face," Parker comments, giving me a nod in the process.

"Rosie and I met here, actually; I guess it was about four or five months ago, right?" I explain, looking to her for confirmation.

"Yes, it's something like that. I literally fell right into his arms," she says, once again beaming up at me.

"Oh man, Mom is going to love this," Tyler teases.

Rolling my eyes, I look over at Rosie. "So, yeah, these are my brothers. They're idiots," I tell her.

Rosie releases a tinkling giggle that sounds sweet to my ears.

"Well, I know about idiot brothers," she jokes. "No offense, guys," Rosie adds as she stands up. "I better get going."

I stand up too, and I kiss her on the corner of her mouth. "I'll pick you up around seven?"

She smiles. "Sounds good." Then she turns to my brothers. "It was really nice to meet you all. I hope to see you again." Turning to me, she says, "I'll see you tonight."

I watch her as she walks away until she disappears through the entrance of the coffee shop.

When I turn around, all three of my brothers are sitting with their elbows on the table and chins in their hands, staring at me with a dreamy look on their faces.

Tyler tries to impersonate a girly voice while saying, "We're dating." He bats his eyelashes.

Then Jasper mocks, "Yes, she fell right into my arms, and I knew she was the one." Loud, booming laughter escapes each of them.

I look at them and shrug.

"You're all assholes, and I don't care what you say. I think I've been waiting for her," I divulge.

Abruptly, their laughter ceases, and none of them says another word until Jasper coughs into his hand and says, "Well, if you put it that way." Then we all finish our coffee in silence.

After my brothers leave, I pull out my laptop. I have work to be done, and I can already see it's going to take everything I have for me to concentrate. All I can think about is Rosie. Her name keeps echoing through my mind, a constant whisper.

My nerves are all over the place because the revelations about my feelings for her keep presenting themselves one after another. I like her. Care about her. Want her. Need her. And it's all of those things that are leaving my head in a state of disarray.

I've been staring at the Google search page for the last few minutes, making no progress on this new proposal.

"Hey there, mate." Andy's voice startles me from my thoughts. Looking over at him, I smile as he takes a seat across from me, setting another black coffee down in front of me. "It seems you and Rosie had that chat we discussed the other day," he continues, taking a long drink of his smoothie he regularly makes for his after-work meal.

A smile creeps across my face. Andy has a way of knowing things, and the fact he was right that day only solidifies he's known Rosie and me better than we've known ourselves.

He sets his drink down on the table and chuckles at my expression.

"I talked to her when she came in, and I noticed her eyes immediately locked on you sitting across the room with your brothers. I knew for sure when I saw the way you both moved around one another and interacted. You're in sync again. I'm thrilled," he explains.

"You're thrilled?" I question, perplexed by his last statement.

"Absolutely, thrilled," he reiterates. "You see, mate, I spend my time looking and enjoying these moments in time as I like to call them. I once told Rosie to enjoy hers, but the thing is I always had a feeling the two of you had more. I like to think of your connection as more of a moment in your lifetime together than just a moment in time."

A lifetime. Am I ready for that kind of prediction? Is that what I want? I don't know. Or at least I don't think I know.

Andy watches me. I know he's reading the emotions that are surely flickering across my face. "I'm not sure where we are when it comes to all of that, Andy, but I can say I like the idea of any moment in time with Rosie. And that alone is something I'm not sure I've ever felt about anyone," I confess.

His gaze lingers on me once the confession is out of my mouth. Something I can't quite decipher crosses his features before he stands up, placing his hand on my shoulder. "Mate, I think you know, but you aren't quite ready to accept the answer. It's going to be a beautiful thing when you do," he declares, then gives my shoulder one last squeeze before walking away.

I watch him go, wondering if Andy is right about the fact I already know the answer to what I ultimately want from Rosie. I worry about what it will take for me to ask for it.

I guess our first date tonight will be the first step in the direction we'll be taking together.

Pivotal moment number three...

*P*ivotal moment number three...the day I realized I might be in over my head.

I'm going to walk over there and beat the shit out of this guy. He's been looking at Rosie all night like she's his possession. Something he wants to own and have his way.

A primal feeling sears my veins as I watch his eyes roam over her body.

When I see her abruptly scoot back in her chair, I know he's touched her beneath the table. I immediately stand. He's going to regret he ever joined that God damned dating site. Before I move, Rosie picks up her purse and leaves the table.

Initially, I keep my eyes glued to Rosie's date as he watches her walk away, turning his head to the side as if he's trying to get a better view of her ass. Again, I contemplate murder.

I catch a glimpse of Rosie darting down the hallway leading to the bathrooms from the corner of my eye. Immediately, my focus changes and I just need to get to her and make sure she's okay.

Following her down the hall, I continue into the bathroom, not caring who else might be in there. When I push the door *open, I spot Rosie instantly. I don't even give her a chance to register the fact I just walked into the ladies' room.*

Taking her face into my palms, I slide my thumb against her cheek. It's so soft. So beautiful.

"Did he touch you?" I ask quietly. What is this girl doing to me? I don't know what I'm going to do if she says yes. I don't know why it even matters, but it does. "Tell me, Rosie. Did he touch you?" I ask, my voice a little more demanding.

Her eyes go wide at my tone. "Drew, barely on my knee, and it doesn't matter," she responds reluctantly.

I have the urge to shout at her that it does matter. It matters to me. But how can I say that to her when I don't even know what that means or if it means anything. It matters to me? It matters.

"It matters," I insist. "He can't do that; it's a rule." Suddenly, I'm peppering kisses all around her mouth. "It's a rule, Rosie," I repeat between kisses.

She closes her eyes, releasing a soft sigh.

That is all it takes for me to lose complete control of my senses. Of its own volition, my mouth covers hers. Something I know now it has wanted to do all day. Losing even more control, my hands and mouth are everywhere. I'm not thinking straight, and Rosie is letting me have my way.

Lifting her, I back her against the wall and slip my hand under her dress, moving toward her most private spot, knowing it's wet and waiting. But this is wrong in here. Doing this to her.

What am I doing? Losing this control? Letting this girl in, letting Rosie in. Rosie.

My God, she deserves better than this. Me practically attacking her in the ladies' room of a restaurant is unacceptable.

Pulling away abruptly, I slowly lower her to the ground.

Pressing my forehead against hers, we both stay in that spot without moving or saying a word. Then it hits me again. She deserves better. She is better.

"Jesus, Rosie. Don't ever let anyone do that to you again. Not me. Not anyone," I tell her before pulling her into my arms, enveloping her. "I'm going insane with want for you. God, how I want you," I whisper.

"Me too," she breathes.

"You owe this guy nothing. Leave," I insist. Then it hits me; I need her, and I'm about to say the craziest thing I've probably ever said. "Hell, you owe me nothing, but I'm going to walk out of this bathroom right now, and I'll be waiting outside your door for you. It will be your decision if you let me in or not."

I don't even wait for an answer from her. I simply turn and walk out of the bathroom.

I don't stop until I reach my car. Once I'm inside, I drop my forehead to the steering wheel. God damn it! I just lost control for the first time in ten years. I'm starting to wonder if this arrangement is such a good idea.

CHAPTER
Eight

It's our first official date. My first date with Rosie. An actual date. More than sex. More than friends, first date. And I'm nervous as hell.

Me. Drew Nallen. The guy all of his friends and family call the playboy is nervous because he's about to go on a real date with a girl. A girl he thinks about constantly. A girl he's falling in love with more and more each time he sees her.

I stand on the bottom step leading up to her apartment building, looking up at the window with that very girl standing in it. She shines, leaning her head out of the window, yelling down, "I'll be right there." Shutting the window quickly, she disappears.

I turn my attention to the doors of her building, waiting for Rosie to appear.

Before I know it, she moves hurriedly through the door, hobbling out with one tall leather boot in her hand and the other on her foot. I look her up and down, my eyes hanging on the way the dark denim hugs her curves. "I couldn't get this damn boot on," she announces just before she stumbles, falling forward into my arms. A quiet yelp slips between her lips. When she hits my chest, I turn her in my arms to cradle her, looking down at her face. Her eyes are closed tightly.

She blinks them open, and without thinking, I press my lips

against hers, unable to resist. Rosie kisses me back, softly caressing my lips with her own. A low moan slips out between our mouths. The kiss is brief yet full of fire, when I force myself to pull away.

Standing her up, I look down into her eyes. "It seems like we just reenacted the first time we met," I joke.

Blushing, Rosie giggles. "I don't think that's exactly what happened the last time I fell into your arms."

"Maybe not, but it's what I thought about doing the first time you fell into my arms." I grin.

She instantly stops laughing, watching me, and I let her for a moment. I want her to understand I'm in this and it's not just some whim or something I decided I suddenly wanted. I want Rosie to grasp the fact I've been thinking about her from the very start.

"Here." I break the silence. "Let me have that boot so I can help you get it on," I insist as I reach for the leather shoe still in her hand.

Rosie hands me the boot and sits on the top step. I move to stand in front of her and hold it out so she can stick her foot in it. When she has her foot in, I push it on with little effort. She shrugs when I stare down at her. I shake my head and smile.

Extending my hand down to her, I pull her up from the steps. "Let's get out of here," I suggest. Rosie nods her head with a smile. I like the way she's looking at me. She looks happy, which only makes me happier.

It's a few blocks to the sushi restaurant; we decide to walk. The night air is cool, but not cold.

At first, we are walking along next to one another, hands at our sides. When I glance over at Rosie, there's a grin on her face. She's looking up at the starlit sky. Again, I'm struck by the look of contentment she's displaying. My heart feels light. I reach over and take her hand in mine. Her eyes dart down to our hands. She doesn't say anything, only stares, then quickly lifts her gaze back to the street in front of us.

"This is okay, right?" I ask her, gesturing toward our entwined hands. "It's not breaking our rule, is it?"

Laughing, she shakes her head. "No, Drew. It's not breaking a rule. Our only rule is we can't be alone when not in public." Her lips tip up on one side. We both know the reason we can't be alone.

Neither of us says a thing the rest of the way to the restaurant.

When we're outside of Shogun, my favorite Japanese place to eat, I stop her. "Here we are, I hope you like sushi," I comment.

"Love it. This is my favorite on the Avenue," she tells me excitedly.

Smiling, I'm glad I chose this place after all. Leading her into the restaurant, I have the waitress sit us in a quiet back corner table. Neither of us needs to look over the menu, and we order several of our favorite rolls each.

"Tell me one thing I don't know about you," she says when the waitress walks away.

Laughing, I look at her likes she's nuts. "Seriously, Rosie? We're doing this?"

"Yes, we're doing this. You promised me real dates. I'm asking real date questions," she insists, a sly grin on her face.

"You're adorable. Do you know that?" I compliment.

"Oh, hell no. Don't call me adorable. No girl wants to be called adorable," she complains. Ironically, she looks super cute doing it, but I get the idea that's not what she'll want to hear.

"Fine, although I don't mean adorable in a negative way at all. I think you're also incredibly gorgeous, funny, and smart. Is that better?" I watch the way her eyes roam over my face, looking for any sign I might be insincere with my compliments. I can see the moment she realizes I'm serious.

Her face turning a deeper shade of red, Rosie reaches her hand across the table and rests it on top of mine. "Drew, that's the nicest thing anyone has ever said to me." Tears hang on the edges of her lids.

A tiny pang in my heart, I lay my other hand on top of hers.

Looking at the emotions on Rosie's face fills me with more of those emotions that have been flooding me since the day I met her. It's becoming clearer I don't stand a chance against this girl.

I make the mistake of walking Rosie all the way up to her door. Neither of us realized the implications of being alone in her hallway. It just isn't public enough.

Because right now, I'm pressing her against the wood of her door, kissing her senseless. Or maybe I'm kissing her until I lose my senses. Because I'm lost. Lost in Rosie. Lost in this feeling she gives me every time our lips meet. Walking her all the way to her door instead of saying our goodnights outside of the building was a really bad idea.

All reason has left her too because Rosie just hiked her leg up and around my waist. Sliding my hand over her thigh, I press into her harder, and a moan slips between our lips. She deepens the kiss and begins reaching for the door knob, and that's when I realize this is a test.

Regardless if she realizes it now, if I allow her to lead us into the apartment and to her bed, this will become everything I'm working hard to steer us away from in this relationship. I want this to be about more than the incredible sex. I want to convince her I want this to become even better than our sex life. I want a relationship built on more.

Pulling my lips from her, I groan. "We made a deal." She blinks at me, her gaze full of desire. "I made you a deal, Rosie. I need to keep it. Not just for you, but I need to keep this bargain because of me. We both have a lot riding on this new arrangement."

Before she can say anything, I press my lips against hers hard and fast, brushing my tongue across her lips and briefly tangling it with hers. Once more, I pull away and quickly turn, walking away from her.

I don't need to turn around to know her hair is mussed, her cheeks are flushed pink, and her body displays every sensation that kiss has left her feeling. I don't need to look because I can feel it. I can feel it when my foot touches the last step outside her apartment. I feel it even after I get home and I close my eyes after I crawl into my bed.

And there's no doubt I'll feel it tomorrow when I open my eyes.

CHAPTER *Nine*

"**S**o Tyler tells me he met your friend, Rosie, and that's she's something to look at," my mom informs me casually as she takes a bite of her Caesar salad.

"Tyler is a dou—" I start to say when I feel Parker kick me under the table and give me the eye. Letting go of my previous urge to berate Tyler, I decide to go to the positive route, or as positive as I can when it comes to my brothers. "Yes, Rosie had the unfortunate privilege of meeting all of the family idiots yesterday. It's so kind of Tyler to share how pretty he feels Rosie is." If my mom notices the sarcasm in my voice, she never lets on. Years of dealing with me and my siblings.

"What do you think, Parker?" my mom asks. She's trying to pull information from us for a reason; I just haven't quite pinpointed why yet. She and I did have the talk the other day about Rosie, but I can see she now has more curiosity in her eyes. What else did Tyler say?

"Mom! I'm sitting right here. Why don't you ask me about Rosie if you want to know about her?" I assert.

"Fine. Tell me more about her," my mom replies then adds, "and I still want to hear what Parker has to say about her." She winks at me. My mother actually winks at me. I drop my head to the table.

Leaning over, I place a kiss to her cheek. "You're relentless, woman." She grins and winks again. I roll my eyes. "Okay, what do you want to know?"

Mom doesn't waste time and jumps right into her questions. "Well, what does she do? Is she from Santa Cruz? How'd did you meet? Because you never said the other day. Is—"

I hold my hand up, and Parker starts laughing. "Mom, let me start with those questions, and you can take a breath," I joke with her.

"Seriously, Mom, you're out of control," Parker says between laughs. This time I kick him under the table. It shuts him up, and he gives me a look like he's going to kick my ass when we're alone. My mom remains seated, eating her lunch and smiling. It's like this whole thing is amusing to her.

"Andrew, I'm waiting," she says, almost giddily.

"Rosie." Simply saying her name causes my chest to burn a little with longing. "She is a copy editor. No, she isn't from Santa Cruz. She's from Texas. We met at The Roasting Company by chance. Or maybe on purpose. Rosie's beautiful and funny and awkward." Rosie is all of these things. What was I doing before her?

"Tyler said you were different around her," she says, interrupting my thoughts.

When I look up, my mom and Parker are watching me. The look on their faces is a cross between happiness and trepidation. I get they aren't used to me reacting this was way about a girl, but this thing with Rosie is different. I'm different, and it's because of her.

Parker speaks up first. "Dude, she seems amazing."

I wait for the but that seems to be lingering in his statement. "She is," I tell them.

"I'm sure she is," my mother adds in. Parker places his elbows on the table. "Drew, man, I just want you to be happy,"

"Don't you think I can decide for myself? I mean, I haven't let a girl in my life this way since Laura. I feel like the fact I'm letting Rosie in means something. I wouldn't be so blasé about this choice. I know what I want," I argue.

"In that case, I can't wait to meet her," my mother offers. "And, you two owe me dessert."

This time she leans over to me and kisses my cheek. "Andrew, we just don't want to see you get hurt again. We love you," she adds.

"I love you guys, too. Now let's get that dessert," I announce.

After we pay the bill and all walk out of the restaurant towards our dessert, I notice Parker's demeanor is a little off from how lunch began. I'll have to ask him about it later.

As we walk with our mom to ice cream heaven, as she likes to call Marianne's, Parker and I discuss our upcoming family get together.

"So are we planning this month's family party together?" I ask Parker, looking ahead of us and noticing we're about to pass the coffee shop.

"Yep, that's the plan," he answers then adds, "Speaking of, are we going with a game night theme?"

My mom starts clapping like a little girl, "Yes! I love that idea!" she says excitedly. Her enthusiasm causes both Parker and me to laugh.

"I don't know, Mom, you know Dad is a cheater when it comes to board or card games. He hates losing," I remind her.

Swatting me on the arm, she scolds me. "Don't say that about your father, even if it is true."

Parker and I bark in laughter.

"Seriously, you two, your father may be a sore loser, but I love game night. I'll talk to him. Plus, it's all in fun," she tries negotiating.

I laugh louder as Parker relents, "Fine, but don't say we didn't try to warn you." This time she slaps him on the arm.

"All of you kids think you're so smart," she remarks.

I'm about to respond when I hear my name called from across the street, diagonal to us. When I glance over, I see Rosie smiling and Abbey rolling her eyes at her side. As soon as the crosswalk signals, they make their way across the street and wait for us to reach them.

I don't take my eyes from her until I hear my mom say, "That's her, isn't it? She's more beautiful than Tyler described.'

Looking over at her, I smile. "Yep, that's her. Don't embarrass me, Mom." I wink at her because I know my mom will do anything but. It's one thing my mom is definitely good about, and that is letting other people carry the conversation and make them feel comfortable.

"Who's that with her?" Parker asks in a strange tone just before we reach Rosie and Abbey.

Abbey must have heard him and his tone because she's reaching her hand out to him. I watch as their eyes lock, neither in what I would call an especially friendly way. "I'm Abbey, the best friend. And you are?"

Parker looks down at her hand then back to her face without accepting her greeting. "I'm Parker, the brother," he replies gruffly.

Looking over at Rosie, I raise my eyebrow in question. She shrugs her shoulders, letting me know she has no clue what just happened between Parker and Abbey. Before swords can be drawn, my mom speaks up. "Parker, don't be rude. I taught you better than that," she scolds lightly as she takes Abbey's hand in hers.

He turns his head and then glances back at Abbey. "My apologies, nice to...meet...you, Abbey." There's still a certain tone to his voice I don't recognize. He quickly directs his attention to Rosie. "Rosie, it's good to see you again. I think I'll run up ahead and grab a coffee before we head to Marianne's. See you all later," he says, taking one last look at Abbey before he walks away.

When I turn my gaze back to Abbey, she's staring after Parker. I'm so confused and will have to remember to ask Parker about this thing we just witnessed between him and Abbey. Abbey turns suddenly and says, "Good to see you, Drew. Mrs. Nallen. I'll see you back at the office, Rosie." Then Abbey dashes down the sidewalk in the same direction as Parker.

"Uh...uh...okay," Rosie replies, although Abbey is too far away to hear her. Turning back to me, she asks, "Do you know what that was all about?"

Shaking my head, I respond, "No idea, but I'll definitely be asking Parks about it later." Looking back in the direction her friend and my brother disappeared in, she remarks, "But there was something...right?"

My mom suddenly chimes in, "Oh, I definitely think there was something."

In the confusion of the encounter between Parker and Abbey, I almost forgot my mom was still standing there. I look at the two women in my life other than my sister and realize they're both watching me expectantly.

"Mom, uh…I…I would like you to meet Rose Fisher. Rosie, this is my mom, Gwen Nallen." I stutter out nervously, although I'm not sure why I'm nervous.

My mom smiles warmly at her as Rosie extends her hand. They take each other's hands in greeting, my mom cradling Rosie's in hers. "Rosie, it's so nice to meet you finally. I've heard so much about you…from all of my boys. You've made quite an impression, especially on Andrew."

Rosie blushes, a pink hue spreading with her grin. "Well, Andrew has made an impression on me, also." She beams, glancing at me from the corner of her eye. It's the first time I've ever heard her say my full name. It sounds sweet and right coming from her lips.

"Well, the boys and I just had lunch and were heading down to Marianne's for a little ice cream. Do you care to join us?" my mother asks, being cordial as usual. "Or rather, would you like to join Andrew and me, because Parker seems to have disappeared on us."

I look expectantly at Rosie. "Do you have time?" I ask, and my mother smacks me on the arm.

"Andrew! That sounded rude." I swallow hard. Looking back at Rosie, I apologize. "You know I didn't mean it that way, right? I just meant, do you have the time or do you need to be back at work soon?"

Shaking her head and laughing, Rosie puts her hand on my arm. "No offense taken, Drew. I knew what you meant, and you're right, I do need to get back to work. Abbey and I were just on our way to grab some coffee before a meeting."

"I'm glad we ran into you, though," I tell her sincerely.

"Yes, Rosie, I'm so glad we ran into you. That you stopped us. I'm just so thrilled to have met you," Mom says. "I'll go see if I can find your brother and let you say goodbye to Rosie without me standing over your shoulder. Rosie, again, it really is nice meeting you and I hope to see you again soon."

"You too, Mrs. Nallen, and I hope so, too," Rosie says sweetly, waving at my mother as she walks away.

"She likes you," I comment.

Rosie turns her attention back to me. "How do you know?" she asks me. "I know because I know my mother. I also know because I don't believe there is anyone who could meet you and not like you," I tell her, taking her hand into mine and rubbing my thumb over her skin absently.

"Are we still on for tomorrow?" I ask her, hoping she hasn't changed her mind.

"Yes, of course," she replies. "Although, I'm a little nervous about your secrecy about where we're going."

I laugh out loud. When I asked her on this date, I told her it would be fun and a surprise. I also told her to wear a bathing suit. She seemed reluctant when she agreed, but I realized it was more about my lack of information than the actual idea of going out with me.

"Don't be nervous. It's going to be fun, I promise," I insist playfully.

"Fine, I trust you, but it better not be dangerous," she teases.

Dangerous? Who does she think I am? Cupping her face, I press my lips lightly to hers. "Rosie, I'd never put you in danger. I promise we're only going to have fun."

She sighs, and I place my lips against hers once more. "Fine," she tells me. " I better get my coffee, find Abbey, and get back to the office."

"Yeah, I better find my mom and Parker. I still wonder what was up between those two earlier," I say, remembering the very distinct reaction my brother had to Abbey. "Anyway, I'll see you tomorrow. Have a good second half of the work day."

"You, too," she responds, squeezing my hand before dashing down the sidewalk and into The Roasting Company.

I watch her and notice the strange tug I feel at my heart every time she leaves me now. It hurts. It's scary. It's also so wonderful that I never want that feeling of wanting her to go away.

Pivotal moment number four...

Pivotal moment number four, when Rosie tried to say goodbye.

She asked me to meet her by the lighthouse. I'm nervous as hell, and I don't know why. Except I think I do. I'm just lying to myself. Pretending. I should admit it. Admit that I'm not only nervous, but I'm scared. Scared of what she is going to say out here in this open space. A place I love and now fear may never see the same again.

I know my fear of the risk is what might destroy me. Ironically, I'm trying to keep myself whole because I fear this time I'll never recover. Maybe, just maybe, I'm holding on to a little more control than things feel at the moment. I'll just keep telling myself that...

When I get out of the car, I already see her standing across the street on the cliff side next to the lighthouse. The sun is about to set, and there's a light breeze blowing. Even from this distance, I can tell she's cold. I watch her a minute. The way the breeze blows lightly at her hair. The way she looks in the light of the setting sun, and it does something to my heart.

As I walk across the street and towards her, I see Rosie

place her hands on the railing along the cliff. She is deep in thought, looking a little sad. Her sadness makes me sad. I know why we're here and I don't want to accept it.

I'm only a few feet away from her when I announce before she turns around, "It's not time." I wait for her to turn around and face me. Even though I can't see her face, I know I took her off guard.

"Drew." My name is carried by the wind when she says it.

I feel as if I might throw up and I feel the need to make her understand it isn't time to end this thing, whatever it is between us. I take her by the shoulders and turn her to face me. "No, Rosie," I beg and repeat, "No, Rosie," once she is looking at me.

Her eyes close and I almost kiss her. I know I can make her feel what I can't seem to admit.

"God, Drew," she sighs, and I can tell she's trying not to cry.

I'm on the verge of tears myself. "Damn it, Rosie! It's not fucking time," I insist desperately. "Open your eyes! Look at me!" I shout because I'm starting to feel angry. I know she doesn't want this to end either. My grip tightens on her shoulders.

When she opens her eyes, tears begin to stream down her cheeks. She shakes her head, and her mouth slightly opens as if she is trying to find the words. Any words that might make this situation better. I know what she's thinking, and I can't give it to her. I can't risk it. And yet, I don't want to let her go even if we did promise to end this arrangement if things ever got hard. And that is exactly what she's trying to do.

Then Rosie is suddenly shouting at me, "Why are you doing this?"

I don't know, *I think.*

She continues, "You promised! You made me swear I would tell you when our arrangement got too hard. I'm trying to tell you, and you won't let me." She sobs. The pain I feel at her words is excruciating.

Pulling her against my chest, I wrap my arms around her. Wanting her to feel it. Please feel it, Rosie. God, please help me. I...I don't know how to do this.

"It's so hard, Drew. It's too hard now. It's time. My time is up." She cries, and I can hear her heart breaking. I wonder if she can hear mine. I've got to find the right words.

"It'll be harder when there is no us," I try telling her.

She pushes against my chest and looks at me. No, don't say it, Rosie. I don't think I can. Don't.

I beg her silently, but she says it. "I need more." Her tears stop coming. "I've been falling slowly...so very slowly in love with you. I want more."

It's exactly what I feared all along. It's the one thing I've told myself I would avoid because love and commitment have never been real for me. My own tears are forming, and the pain inside grows because I just can't do what she wants. "I can't do more," I whisper.

It's strange because when those words I've said a thousand times leave my mouth, I instantly know they're a lie. Ironically, a lie is the reason I've never let myself do more than casual. She knew I was going to say those words; I can see it on her face.

And it's confirmed when she says, "I know, and that's why it's time."

When she rises on her tiptoes, I lower my lips over hers lightly. It's the moment I can no longer keep my tears at bay. We don't move. We stay connected by this soft, gentle kiss. We savor it. I never want to move because I know she intends for this to be our last. I won't be the first to pull away. I can't.

That's when I feel her slowly take a step back. No. "Please..." I say in a quiet plea. I want to say more, but the fear takes over. The what ifs. When I look at her, I can tell she's hesitating, waiting for me to continue. To change my mind. What she doesn't understand is she's asking the impossible of me.

Shrugging, she pushes her shoulders back, wipes away her tears, and turns and leaves. She doesn't look back. I make one last effort. "Don't leave me. I can't," I plea. She still doesn't turn around. And I still don't tell her I want more.

Even when I feel my heart leave with her.

CHAPTER Ten

"**P**addle! Paddle! Keep paddling, Rosie! Dip!" I shout at her as we rise and dip with the waves as we make our way off shore. She's lying across the top of the board in front of me on my longboard. It's been forever since I've taken my longboard out; it's not really my thing anymore, but I knew if I wanted to take Rosie out and get her up, then this board is ideal.

"I am! I can't believe you talked me into doing this," she yells back over the sound of the waves rolling past us. I can hear both the excitement and nerves in her voice. "I'm not going to be able to do this."

I smack her on the ass and resume paddling as she releases a startled screech. "You will, but not if we don't make it past the break, now dip." We dip the board beneath the wave and continue to paddle.

When we finally reach the spot I was hoping for, I tell her to stop paddling. "So now what?" she asks, pushing herself up and straddling the board. I follow suit and place my legs on either side of the board, too. I scoot myself closer to Rosie, my chest pressing against her back.

Moving my lips close to her ear, I whisper, "We wait." I feel her shiver, but I don't think it's from the cold air around us.

"We wait," she breathes. This time I'm the one who shivers.

Remembering where we are and what I brought her out here to do,

I begin to explain. "It's all about instinct. You feel the rhythm of the water. You clear your mind, concentrate. Do you think you can do that?"

Nodding her head, Rosie laughs. "I think I'd have a better chance of concentrating without you pressed up against me."

Shaking my head, I sigh. "You don't know just how true those words are."

Just when I decide we should forget about this surfing thing and paddle back in to break every rule I put into place with our new arrangement, I feel it. The ripple of the water passes us, then the sound of the approaching wave.

"This is it," I tell her.

"This is it?" she questions, breathy.

"Rosie, you're about to surf. Now lay forward and start paddling, feel it, and listen for my cue and don't forget to pop up." She nods her head as she moves her body forward and starts paddling. I move with her, and together we push ourselves forward, ahead of the wave perfectly. "Feel that?"

Rosie nods her head.

"Now," I yell over the moving water.

Together we pop up onto our feet. Once we have our balance, we sail across the water. I can hear Rosie giggling. "Oh my God!" she screams, her laugh vibrating through my body as I move forward on the board and wrap my arms around her as we reach the end of the wave.

I pull her over and into the water, cradling her against me. A yelp sounds through the air just before we hit the water.

When we break the surface again, she's spluttering water and laughing at the same time. My own chest vibrating with happiness, I lift her up as she wraps her arms around my neck.

"That was amazing." She smiles and presses her lips hard against mine.

"You're amazing," I say against her lips then take the kiss deeper. We're now pressed into the sand, the tide washing up around us. "Rosie, we're pretty incredible, too. Together."

Rolling her on top of me, she smiles as she looks into my eyes.

"Yeah, we are. Thank you for this day," she agrees. Her joy is shining in the look she's giving me. It's everything I want her to feel.

"The sun may be going down, but the day isn't quite over," I remind her, a grin spreading across my face.

We're sitting quietly on one of the dedication benches, snuggled close, a cool breeze coming off the ocean. Rosie stares out over the ocean as my eyes focus on her. This moment is reminiscent of a day not so long ago. A day I'd rather forget, but definitely one that changes me completely.

"Being at this lighthouse brings up feelings I don't really like remembering," I disclose to her, breaking the silence around us.

"I was just thinking the same thing," she admits just before she turns her attention to me.

"I'm so sorry I was such a coward, Rosie," I apologize.

Her eyes shimmer with unshed tears. Tilting her head slightly, Rosie shakes her head. "No, Drew. Don't apologize anymore. There is nothing to apologize for because you had your reasons." Shrugging, she leans forward, softly pressing her lips to mine briefly then continuing, "Maybe one a day you'll tell me what kept you from letting people in and what finally changed your mind."

Those words should've been the opening to do exactly what she just said. They should've let me know she wanted to know. That I can trust her with the one thing I've kept shut off...my heart. I should've told her it was her who tore down the wall I spent so much time building. Building because of Laura and the fact her lies broke my trust and the innocence of my heart a long time ago.

Instead, the words stay lodged in my throat, and I pull her hard against me. My body quivers, shaking both of us. I'm holding Rosie so tight, trying to make her feel what I can't seem to form the words to say.

Just like the last time we were here on this cliffside overlooking the sea, full of possibilities. A moment for us to move forward. A time for me to move past the lies from another lifetime and start new with a girl who has nothing to do with the hurt from years ago. It's my opportunity.

Pulling back from me, Rosie looks into my eyes. She doesn't say anything, only stares, like she is trying to see what I'm not telling her. Then she pecks me lightly, pulls back again, and says, "Don't, okay? This isn't like last time we were here. I'm not done. It's not time, and more than anything, I'm not finished." She places her lips against mine again and lingers a little longer this time before looking into my eyes again. "I don't think you're finished either. You're not ready to tell me, and I'm okay with that. This wasn't part of the rules. Opening yourself to the possibility of what we can and could be is the only rule. I don't need the other now. I don't need your past hurts. I only want your future happiness. What do you say?"

My God, this girl. This beautiful, sweet, and honest woman.

Placing both of my hands on either side of her face, I pull her mouth swiftly to mine. I kiss her hard, and passionately. My heart is mending, becoming whole again and beating more freely with every second I spend with Rosie.

Someday I'll be able to say all the things I've kept locked away. I'll say them to her because she is the one who has the key. She's the one who has my heart, and as she deepens the kiss, I can feel that I have hers, too.

CHAPTER *Eleven*

A few days later, Rosie and I walk through the same door where we first met.

"Rosie. Drew, mate. It's lovely to see you this morning," Andy greets us as we walk up to the counter to place our order. We agreed to meet for coffee before work this morning. We've been trying to change things up, and it's been a while since we've been in here together.

"Good morning," Rosie and I respond to Andy's greeting simultaneously. Andy gives us both an approving grin. He has been in our corner from the beginning, so I'm not surprised to see his cheery disposition at seeing the two of us together.

"How have things been?" he continues the conversation.

Again, we both say, "Good." Then we start laughing.

"You know, this is getting kind of ridiculous that I never order something new. It's always the same, and to think I was trying to be bolder only a few months ago. What was I thinking when I can't even try a new coffee drink?" Rosie says, giggling.

I shrug my shoulders as I pay for our coffees. "What does your taste in coffee have to do with who you are as a person?"

"Yes, Rosie. Most people come in every day and order the same drink, but if you want, next time I will make a suggestion," Andy adds before looking at the next person in line.

Once we grab our drinks, our eyes roam over the room for an available table.

Sitting at their usual table is the dynamic five. Lynn notices us first and shouts, "Rosie and Drew in the house!"

Lenny lifts his cup in acknowledgment. Lorna only turns and smiles, then directs her attention back to the conversation she is having with Lenny. Colleen waves wildly. Jumping out of her chair, Marti comes running over to us, throwing her arms around Rosie's neck. "Hey, you two. We've been missing you both," she says candidly just before she pulls me into a quick hug.

"I've missed seeing you, too. Work has been crazy, and when I have come in you haven't been here," Rosie tells her. "I'm glad I saw you today." She's so sweet and sincere.

"Yes, well, I have been in and out. Anyway, I won't keep you two. I just wanted to say a quick hello and give you a squeeze," Marti tells us. "See you soon." She walks away and joins the conversation of the table like she never left.

Looking over to Rosie, I nod my head toward a table in the corner. "How about that one over there?"

"Perfect," she responds, leading the way to the table I pointed out to her.

After we take a seat, we start chatting.

"Do you have plans this weekend?" Rosie asks, blowing on her latte. I watch the way her lips purse when she blows, and it's adorable.

"Will you be mad if I tell you how adorable you are?" I ask her, already expecting the wrath I've experienced by way of the daggers shooting from her eyes.

Rolling her eyes, she grumbles, "What could I have possibly done in the last thirty seconds to make you feel the need to call me adorable?"

"You existing period is adorable. In fact, if I were to look up adorable in the dictionary, your picture would be next to it with *see picture* in italics below it," I tease her.

Her eyes go wide then she explodes with laughter, coffee shooting from her mouth and onto my face.

"Oh my God!" she shouts, covering her mouth with her hand.

My eyes are closed. I can feel the drops of liquid rolling down my face. I listen as Rosie scrambles to her feet then begins rubbing my face with napkins, trying to dry me off.

Then she's laughing again, so hard, I can barely understand her when she says, "How adorable do you think I am now?"

Without warning, I grab her around the waist, pulling her onto my lap. Rubbing my wet face all over her, pressing kisses around her mouth until I finally plant a hard lingering one to her lips. We both freeze. I forgot where we were and I think she forgot too. Both of us got caught up in the moment, in the easy way being together is for us.

"Drew? Do you think people are looking at us?" she whispers without taking her eyes away from mine.

I allow my eyes to roam around the room; I haven't met one set of eyes looking our way. Well, that is until my gaze connects with Andy. He's smiling brightly and shaking his head. Then he mouths the words, *"Moments in time."*

"Nope, It's just you and me," I tell her, placing another soft kiss to her lips.

Later that night when I walk through the door to my apartment, I throw my bag down on the floor near the couch. Pulling out my phone, I decide to take care of something that's been on my mind all day.

Drew: *Yo, Parks! I think I'm going to invite Rosie to the family game night on Saturday.*
Parker: *Dude! Are you fucking kidding me?*
Drew: *No, is it a problem? You don't think Mom and Dad will care, do you?*
Parker: *Nope. No issue, just surprised, man. As for Mom and Dad, they won't give a shit. In fact, Mom will be so excited that*

maybe she'll lay off me about girls.
Drew: *Oh, yeah, that reminds me. What was up between you and Rosie's friend, Abbey the other day? Do you know her?*
Parker: *Not happening.*
Drew: *What's not happening?*
Parker: *I'm not talking to you about that. Just let it go, Dude.*
Drew: *Fine, but be nicer next time. She is Rosie's best friend, after all.*
Parker: *Ask Rosie about the party. See you on Saturday.*
Drew: *Yeah, see you on Saturday.*

Tossing the phone on the couch next to me, I get up, heading for the kitchen to make something to eat. Once I make a sandwich, I take my plate back to the couch with me. Setting it on the coffee table, I pick my phone back up, taking a deep breath.

Asking Rosie to a family get-together. It's a big deal. It's like no matter how slow I intend to go, everything moves at warp speed when it comes to Rosie and me. I mean, it was just a short time ago, you wouldn't even catch me putting Rosie and me together. It was today at The Roasting Company that the thought of inviting her first crossed my mind. It's been nagging me all day. I want her there with me. With my family.

Drew: *Hey, Adorable. You around?*

I eat my food while I wait for a response. It's a few minutes before I get a reply.

Rosie: *Who is this?*
Drew: *Seriously?*
Rosie: *Well, I don't know. Are you seriously calling me adorable again?*
Drew: *I only speak truths.*
Rosie: *No.*
Drew: *Fine. What are you doing?*

Rosie: *I'm on the couch, watching television with Abbey.*
Drew: *I'm jealous.*
Rosie: *You should be, she's feeding me Chunky Monkey and giving me all of the banana chunks.*
Drew: *That Abbey is an amazing friend. Speaking of Abbey, did you ever ask her about the weirdness between her and Parker?*
Rosie: *Yes, she wouldn't spill and tried playing it off. Something is going on, but I got nothing. Did you ask Parker?*
Drew: *Yep, and I basically got the brush-off, too. Oh well, that's not why I'm texting anyway.*
Rosie: *Oh? So what are you texting me about?*
Drew: *Actually, are you leaving the house tonight?*
Rosie: *Uh, I wasn't planning on it.*

Before I answer her, I'm up off the couch and out the door. I've decided I want to ask her in person. What a jackass move to ask her out by text. She deserves more than that, and honestly, this isn't a regular date.

Rosie: *Hello? Where did you go?*

Thank God we only live a few blocks from one another because running there just wouldn't be as easy. Or quick.

Rosie: *Seriously, Drew?*

When I make it to her building, I run to the elevator. I don't want to tell her I'm coming over. I want to surprise her.

Rosie: *Drew!!! Where did you go?*
Drew: *I'm here.*
Rosie: *What the heck? Why'd you leaving me hanging like that?*
Drew: *I had to go somewhere.*
Rosie: *Where?*
Drew: *Here*

Rosie: *What?*
Drew: *I'm here.*
Drew: *At your door.*

A few seconds pass and the door swings open. I place the biggest grin on my face.

"Drew! What in the ever-loving hell are you doing here?" she exclaims, her eyes wild as she touches her messy bun.

"Man, you're right," I say, a bit dumbfounded.

"I am?" she questions, looking confused by my comment.

"You're right. You aren't adorable at all," I tell her, allowing my eyes to roam over the bare, smooth skin of her face.

"Well, I didn't know you were coming over!" she shouts this time.

"Rosie, you didn't let me finish. What I meant is, you're not adorable. You're breathtaking. You're beautiful. You are more than adorable," I admit, devotedly.

"Oh." She blushes.

"Yeah. Okay, I didn't run all the way over here to tell you that, though, although I'm glad I did. What I wanted to say, or rather what I want to ask you is, would you like to come with me to my family's game night on Saturday?" I stumble over my words.

"Uh…you want me to come with you to your family party?" she says, almost in a whisper.

"I know I didn't ask very eloquently, but yes, that's exactly what I was trying to ask you," I affirm.

The smile that lights up her face is so bright, I can't help the one that forms on mine.

"Are you sure?" she asks.

"Of course I am," I tell her.

"Really?" she says giddily.

Abbey's voice rings out from somewhere behind her in the apartment. "Damn it, Rosie! Say yes already so you can get your sweet ass back in here, and I can continue to drool over Four."

We both start laughing, and Rosie shrugs her shoulders. "Movie night," she tells me then continues, "Yes, I would love to go with you."

"Thank you," I breathe. An uncontrollable smile forms on my face once more.

I quickly pull her in for a short, searing kiss. One I don't want to stop, but know I need to and I need to stop right now. When we pull apart, I immediately turn and run back home, feeling light. Feeling like I just took another giant leap in this relationship instead of the baby steps I intended to take all along.

CHAPTER
Twelve

Holding hands, Rosie and I make our way down the pathway leading to my parents'. The door swings open with my mom waiting to greet us. "Rosie. Andrew. We're so happy you made it." Her voice is cheerful and full of her typical energy.

Rosie beams. "Mrs. Nallen." My mom is pulling her in for a gentle hug. That woman isn't all that familiar with personal space. Luckily, I'm confident Rosie doesn't mind.

"Mom, of course we made it. I'm the one who planned the shindig," I tease. She kisses me on the cheek as I pass her.

"Drew, stop it. I'm just nice. Now take Rosie in to meet your father. He's in the family room. You guys are the first to arrive," Mom tells us as she shuts the door and leaves us to head upstairs. "I'll be back down in a minute."

I take Rosie's hand again and start to lead her down the short hall to the family room. Just before we turn the corner within sight of my dad, I stop Rosie, pulling her to me. She looks up at me questioningly. I caress her cheek with my thumb. "I just wanted you for a moment longer to myself because once we walk in there, and my brothers and sister arrive, we won't have a moment alone." I touch my mouth to hers, softly. "I want to apologize ahead of time for all of them because they have no idea what personal space is or realize when they cross a line, except for maybe Parker. I love them all, but we forget that all families aren't like our family. Are you sure about this? I can make an excuse."

She squeezes her arms tighter around my waist, smiling. "Drew, I'm good. And you haven't met my family. I'm used to loud and filterless banter. Let's do this."

"Okay, but don't say I didn't warn you," I say, still unsure. Holding Rosie close a moment longer, I add, "Oh, and by the way, I really, really like you, Rose Fisher."

Her smile brightens the whole room. "And I really, really like you, Andrew Nallen."

Letting her out of my embrace, I take her hand and walk into the family room. We find my dad sitting in the big, overstuffed beige chair in the corner, reading a magazine. He looks up over his glasses when we enter the room.

"Drew." My dad sets the magazine down and stands, giving me a hug, then turns his attention to Rosie. "You must be the Rose everyone is talking so much about," he remarks, extending his hand in greeting.

"Oh, uh, I guess that would be me, and you must be the one and only Mr. Nallen," she says, sounding completely in her element and accepting his greeting.

Things I now know about Rosie: while she may be awkward and klutzy on occasion, there are some situations she handles better than most, especially if she is comfortable.

Chuckling, my dad looks over at me. "I like her already." Then he takes a seat. "Drew, get dinner set up in the kitchen and our guests something to drink while you're at it. Your mother said she laid everything out for you. Parker dropped off the feast you guys have planned for tonight earlier in the day. I'll keep this lovely lady company while we wait for the others to get here."

Glancing over at Rosie, she nods to let me know she's fine. "Sure, Dad. No embarrassing stories," I joke, winking at Rosie.

As I walk away and out of the room, I can hear my dad asking Rosie about her family. There is a slight tug at my heart because it's a nice feeling my parents already feel comfortable with Rosie. I don't worry about the need to keep Rosie company when I begin to prepare dinner.

In fact, I feel pretty damn great until I hear the slamming of the front door and the loud, arguing voices of my two younger brothers. Poor Rosie may change her mind about feeling comfortable with those two bozos around.

Laughter erupts around the table as Rosie meets Tyler's bet and raises it ten dollars. Tyler yells, "Bullshit!" and everyone laughs harder. Rosie's expression remains neutral. Leaning over, I press my mouth close to her ear and whisper, "You're a shark."

"God damn it, Drew! No whispering in her ear," Tyler shouts, sounding annoyed.

"Tyler James Nallen! You better watch your mouth," my mom scolds in her usual, futile attempt at getting one of us to refrain from cursing. My dad pats her hand and rolls his eyes, letting her know he thinks she's ridiculous for trying to threaten Tyler.

"Quit acting like a little ass, Tyler, and make your move," Kelsea says in my defense.

"Fine," he grumbles, glancing at his cards then tossing his chips in a pile.

Rosie doesn't even flinch. She takes a casual peek at her hand. Everyone is quiet around the table until Jasper says, "Drew, I may be falling for your girl."

I kick Parker under the table, and he punches Jasper in the shoulder. "Ow, you two are such assholes," he cries. I give Parker a high five across the table.

"You all are a bunch of heathens. Rosie will never want to come over here again," Dad comments as Mom rests her head on his shoulder.

"Okay, let's see your showdown," I tell them both after the river card is shown.

Rosie and Tyler each flip their cards over.

"Four of a kind, queens," Rosie brags.

Tyler looks at his full house and blows out a long breath. "Fuck." Parker, Jasper, and Kelsea all whoop and holler, teasing Tyler. Mom and Dad clap their hands.

Standing up, I tug Rosie out of the chair and into an embrace. She's laughing and so am I. I kiss her on the side of her head and set her down. She immediately turns toward Tyler, who's sitting with his head down while he flips our brothers and sister off.

"Tyler, you are a worthy adversary," she acknowledges, her eyes shining with humor.

Looking up at her, Tyler grins. "I guess I should've known better than to think I could beat a Texas girl at Texas Hold'em."

Rosie winks and starts clearing the table while everyone else bursts into laughter. Mom jumps up and starts clearing the table alongside her, shouting, "You guys better get your butts in gear and start cleaning up. We aren't letting Rosie clean up this mess all on her own."

As a family, we all start carrying plates and glasses to the kitchen, chatting, laughing, and joking like on any other family night. At one point, I notice Rosie standing in the doorway of the kitchen, watching everyone. Walking up behind her, I press into her back. "Whatcha doin?" I ask her in a low voice.

She doesn't answer, only reaches her hand down and behind her to take hold of mine. "Watching your family. It makes me miss home a little, but it also makes me feel good because they've all been so welcoming."

Turning her to face me, I look into her eyes. "Rosie, you're amazing. They love you, and if you can accept their crazy, then you can spend every family get-together with us if you want," I tell her without thinking. I only think about how I'm feeling at that very moment with her and not about my words. Not about the weight they carry.

I realize after a few minutes that Rosie hasn't said anything; she's only staring at me. There's a surprised gleam in her eye, like she's unable to determine how she should take what I just said. I decide to give her something else to think about and place a quick kiss to her lips. I step around her and go help Kelsea dry and put away the dishes without looking back.

CHAPTER Thirteen

After all the dishes are dry, I go off in search of Rosie. I haven't seen her since I left her standing in the doorway twenty minutes ago. She couldn't have gone far. I hear my dad, brothers, and Kelsea in the family room arguing over who's the greatest soccer player of all time. *Pele, of course,* I think at the same time Parker announces it out loud. I chuckle to myself.

I notice the string lights on the porch are on, dimly lighting the back, giving me the ability to see two silhouettes standing side by side with their backs to me, looking out over the backyard.

Quietly, I walk through the doorway without their notice and just before I approach them, I hear my mother say my name.

"Rosie, I really like you, and I hope you don't think I'm one of those mothers who butt into their kids' lives when I ask you if you're sure about how you feel for Andrew." Mom turns her head toward Rosie, and Rosie continues looking straight forward.

"I would never presume to know what it's like to be a mother. I imagine you just want to protect him. All of your kids. So, no, I don't think that at all," Rosie tells her honestly. Sighing, she continues, "As for how I feel about Drew, I haven't even really told him. We haven't told one another. Things have been complicated between us. It's no one's fault but our own."

"Complicated. How very Andrew-like," my mom comments, a slight humor to her tone.

"Yeah, well, I'm no better," Rosie remarks. "And, I'm the one who brought Drew into our complication. I think things were pretty simple for him before I came along. I care about Drew. A lot. He's so unlike anyone I've known, and I feel so comfortable...at home when he's around."

A smile drifts across my features as I eavesdrop on them. I find it humorous Rosie takes so much responsibility for our situation.

"Well, Drew had his battle with complicated a long time ago. I don't want to see him get hurt..." Mom is saying. I quickly make my presence known before she can say anything else.

"Hey, you two, what's happening out here?" I interrupt.

"Oh, honey, I was just getting to know Rosie a little better and maybe I was also trying to give her a break from your brothers." Mom walks toward me, kissing me on the cheek. In a whisper, as she walks past me, she tells me, "Be brave. She's a keeper."

I quickly peck her on the cheek, letting her know I heard her words.

"So, my mom," I say to Rosie once I reach her.

She laughs lightly. "She's great," Rosie says genuinely. "I really like her."

"Good, and I think she really likes you." I wrap my arms around her shoulder and pull her gently toward me. She leans her head on my shoulder. It feels nice. "Again, thank you for coming tonight."

Lifting her head and facing me, Rosie touches her lips to mine. "You don't need to thank me. I should be thanking you for inviting me." Her lips meet mine again. They're warm and soft, gently prodding my lips apart. I wrap her in my arms as our mouths move against one another in a sensual kiss.

When we finally pull apart, I rest my forehead against hers and inhale softly. Her scent is calming me, yet at the same time creating a yearning for her I promised us both wouldn't happen until we were both ready.

"I better get you home," I tell her. "Especially because if we don't leave now, someone is bound to talk us into playing another round of Texas Hold'em.

"Yeah, I'm not sure Tyler can take losing to me twice in one night," she jokes, walking away. A loud laugh escapes me as I slap her on the ass and she yelps.

Dating Rosie Fisher is too much fun.

The outside of Rosie's apartment is dimly lit, and the usual fog hangs in the buildings and lampposts. The chill in the air clings to us and I feel her shiver. Quickly, I pick Rosie up and rush up the steps, a surprised scream coming from her, and then a giggle.

"What are you doing?" she exclaims between laughs.

"I'm getting you inside more quickly, Ms. Fisher," I tell her, setting her down just inside the building foyer.

She holds her hands out to me, fingers white. "So cold...I can't feel my fingers," she chatters. I take her hands between mine, cupping them and blowing my warm breath on them. "It isn't that cold." I laugh. She shakes her head in disagreement, and I grin.

"Okay, get upstairs and into the warmth of your own home," I suggest. I pull her into a heated kiss. It is never easy to leave her, but tonight feels especially hard. I'm not sure if it's the time we spent with my family tonight alone or all of our dates combined, but I feel so connected to Rosie. Something I never expected when we began all of this together.

Pushing her back, I give her one last peck on the cheek. Rosie looks as dazed as I feel.

"Good night, Rosie. Thank you for tonight. In fact, thank you for giving me this second chance," I tell her, hoping she can feel and hear the sincerity in my voice.

"Stay," she states so quietly I almost miss it.

"What?" I ask, nervous.

"I said stay with me," she repeats, her voice a little louder. A little more sure.

Grabbing her shoulders, I pull her against me, squeezing her in a tight embrace because a war is raging between what I want to do and what I think I should do. I'm worried she's only asking because of the moment instead of what she really wants to happen between us.

If I stay, it means we are done with this new arrangement. We are saying this is bigger than what's happened between us so far. At least that is what it will mean for me. Is she sure? Am I?

As hard as it is for me to get the words out, I close my eyes and reply, "I can't. This is against our rules."

"Oh." She sounds so hurt. Maybe even a little shocked by my reply. Kissing me on the cheek, she sputters out, "Thank you for tonight. It was amazing. Fun." She quickly turns on her heels and heads to the open elevator. I'm frozen. Watching her go and trying to decide why she said a hasty goodbye. Why she sounded so hurt.

We stare at one another until the elevator doors close, and I'm left standing alone.

I remain in that spot, going over everything for an undetermined amount of time. Thinking of every moment that led us here, to me standing in the foyer of Rosie's building, staring at elevator doors. Feeling sure and conflicted at the same time. I'm still afraid, but this time I'm not afraid of being with her. I'm afraid of making a choice that will leave me without her.

My rational brain kicks in. She asked me up. Maybe Rosie is feeling the same thing as I am, yet she took a chance and asked me to stay. She's ready to take a real chance on me. I want that real chance.

Rushing up to the elevator, I hit the button to her floor over and over because it can't get here quick enough. The doors open and I step in; I have no more than a minute to figure out exactly what I'm going to say to Rosie to convince her I want to stay and what this means for me. For us.

And hopefully, for her.

Pivotal moment number five...

*P*ivotal moment number five happened when I couldn't find the right words.

I'm an ass. Even if it weren't completely true, I definitely made an ass of myself. When I saw Rosie walk into the restaurant with that Travis guy, I'd never been as devastated and pissed off at the same time as I was at that moment.

As you can guess, that isn't the best combination for good decisions.

It's the reason I didn't consider how my actions and reactions would affect Rosie. I was selfish as usual. Now, I'm standing here, in our coffee shop, in the spot we first introduced ourselves to one another, and she's angry with me.

"Drew, what the hell was all of that?" she inquires, her voice full of anger. God, I am so damn sorry. I can see what I've done to her now, but I have no idea what to say to make her understand. I don't know how to answer her question. I don't know exactly what I'm doing.

So I say the first thing that comes to my mind. "When did it get so hard to breathe around you?"

I see the moment my question turns her anger into confusion.

She whispers, "I don't know what you mean."

My frustration grows, with her, with myself. "Damn it, Rosie. This wasn't what I intended to happen. I don't do this," I say, waving my hand at us. "This doesn't happen to me. I have everything I want. I don't want more...I didn't want more.

Of course she's confused, because I'm confused myself.

"Drew, I...I don't know what you're saying. This is exactly what was supposed to happen. This was our plan...our deal," she sounds desperate, and again I feel angry. Not at her, but with myself. With Rosie, I'm aggravated she can't see everything I see.

"No! No, you're wrong. This isn't what we planned. This isn't the deal I made. My life was supposed to stay controlled. I was supposed to walk away, and my life was supposed to continue turning on its normal axis, but then..."

I pause in my little monolog and sit on the one chair left right side up. I put my elbows on my knees and my face in my hands. I feel so out of control; I'm sick. I'm nervous and so full of fear that I'm going to lose this and never survive, yet I fear the consequence of allowing her all the way in. The ironic thing is I think she's already all the way in.

"Drew, I..." I hear her start to say.

I can't let her say it. I can't take the chance of what she might say.

Abruptly, I stand up. "Don't, Rosie." My voice sounds off,

and I know it, but I continue anyway, "You have no idea." A laugh escapes me, but there isn't anything humorous. My back is to her, and I suddenly feel her lightly touch my shoulder. I shiver. "You wanted me to teach you to be more confident. To be a person who is noticed. The ironic thing is, Rosie…" I whip around and face her, her hand falling from my shoulder. I continue, "The most laughable thing is you were always noticeable. From the moment I saw you dashing down the sidewalk in the rain, I knew it. When I caught you in my arms and peered into your whiskey-colored eyes, I was sure of it."

I can see I'm scaring her. My words are scaring her because she's afraid to hope for what they might mean. She's afraid to believe in what they might mean. I'm afraid too, but I keep going.

"I've never met anyone who only had to walk into a room to so naturally and unintentionally command the attention of everyone in it. You touch people with a simple glance. They fall more under your spell with every awkward word that slips past your lips. I know I did. This is why I should've known when you asked me to be a part of this charade; I should've turned you down. That the moment I touched you, I mean really touched you, I would be ruined forever. But I was cocky. Arrogant. I made the stupid mistake of pretending you were like any other girl. The mistake of pretending I could walk away from this unchanged and back to my old life."

After my little speech, I can see all of the emotions drift over

Rosie's features. Excitement. Fear. Doubt. I dare to hope.

"I think I fell...I think I may want more," I tell her, still fearful of being completely open.

For some reason, this last statement changes something. She takes a step back. I'm not sure what I said exactly, but it was definitely something that just gave her pause. Suddenly, a loud laugh escapes. "You think? Did you just end all of that with you think you may want more?" she says angrily.

I flinch. I wasn't expecting her anger. I didn't mean it the way it sounded to her. I meant I do.

"Rosie, that's not..." I start to tell her.

"Oh, that's not what you meant?" she spits. She puts her hand up when I start to defend my words. "You're wrong. You're so very wrong. This is the exact purpose of our deal. I'm smarter about relationships. I'm more confident in who I am...more experienced. You were supposed to get your kicks and walk away, back to your fun, uncommitted bachelor life. You told me I couldn't want more and I held up my end of the bargain."

She's got it all wrong, I reach for her, but she moves out of my reach, and I take two more steps toward her, keeping my hands at my side. "You don't mean this...you have to know," I try explaining, but it just isn't coming out right.

"I do mean it," she says.

"I won't accept it," I respond stubbornly.

She smiles a very un-Rosie like smile. I hate it. Placing her *hand on the side of my face, she barely chokes out, "We were never meant to be more than this. Accept it, Drew." She swallows then gives one final blow. "I have."*

She stares at me for one more brief second before turning and walking away. She may be fooling herself, but I'm done playing games with my own heart. For the first time in years, I want more.

CHAPTER *Fourteen*

I changed my mind. She looks at me warily as if I broke another promise. Like I broke her heart again. She thinks I'm still scared, but Rosie's wrong. I'm not scared of how I feel. Or of how I hope she feels.

I had a momentary lapse of judgment when it came to deciding if it's time. Not time to end things, but time to move forward. I didn't want her to feel pressured; it's the only reason I hesitated about coming in.

"Rosie, it's not what you think," I say to her as she stares at me from the other side of the threshold. I know I need to say more. I need to be clear. "I didn't want you to feel pressured, so for a moment, I thought it was better if I didn't stay, but then I realized I was wrong. There are things I need to say to you. Things I should've said a long time ago. Can I please come in?"

There is a momentary silence between us where neither of us takes our eyes off the other. Slowly, Rosie opens the door wider to allow me in.

Once she closes the door, I swivel around, and without hesitation, I lay out my heart before her. "The day you fell into my arms, I fell right with you. From that day and every day after, I was falling. Falling so quickly, I never had time to get my bearings." I take a deep breath so she can catch up to what I'm trying to tell her then continue, "You see, I didn't trust anyone enough to let them in. I have my reasons. I was hurt. I was lied to and made to believe what I am isn't who I should be. I was just like you. And just like with you, they were wrong. We were wrong ever to feel that way because we were fucking perfect the way we were. The way we are. You never need to change. You captured my attention the moment I saw you. We're even better together."

Taking a step forward, I watch her tear-filled eyes brighten. She's starting to accept what I'm trying to tell her.

"I'm sorry it took me so long to figure things out. I'm sorry I hurt you, but I promise I will never do it again," I vow, pulling her to me and placing my lips over hers. She kisses me back, and I feel my heart become whole.

Pulling back, I look down at her. "I want a new deal. I want you. Only you. I want dates. I told you once I was going to like kissing you regularly. That's what I want. I want to kiss you regularly. I want the late-night snuggles. And the mornings after. I want it all with you," I confess to her.

Rosie's face lights up. "Are you sure you can handle this kind of arrangement? I'm not sure this is your kind of thing," she teases, a smile wide on her face.

"I can, and it is," I reply. "The question is, are you sure you want to risk making this deal with me?"

Rosie shakes her head and rolls her eyes. "Is that even a question? Drew, I've been waiting for you. I know I promised not to fall in love with you, but I did. I only stepped back because I wanted it to be real. I wanted it to be permanent. I wanted you to be sure about what you were feeling."

"I've never been surer about anything in my life," I confess.

Rosie takes my hand and leads me toward her bedroom. I pull her to a stop just before we get to the doorway. "Rose, we don't have to do this now. We have plenty of time."

She grabs me by the front of my shirt and yanks me through the door. "I know, and I'm ready to get started on this new kind of more, now." I wasn't expecting her to pull me so hard and we both start stumbling. I wrap my arm around her waist and help steady the both of us.

Her body now flush against mine, I can feel every inch of her curvy body pressed against me. It feels good. Right.

A surge of lust moves through me, and I can't wait another second to have my lips on her.

She comes willingly, matching my own need to be closer. The last month has been torture, keeping my feelings at bay, pushing aside my desire for Rosie so I could prove to her I want more than the physical relationship we started months ago.

I want to savor her, worship her, so I slow my movements, kissing her softer yet deeper. "Rose, I want to go slow, I don't want to rush." Without a word, she pulls me gently closer. Her hands move under my T-shirt, lifting the hem of it. I raise my arms until it's all the way off. She runs her soft hands down my chest and places her lips against the skin of my ribs.

We slowly peel away every barrier between us until we are standing inches apart with nothing but a burning desire. I take her in my arms, pushing away every doubt, every deceit, every unkind word or broken commitment before we found one another.

I caress her face, and she leans into the palm of my hand, closing her eyes. I can't take my eyes away from her. This girl who rescued me. Who gave me a reason to be the person I really am.

"I fell in love with you, Rosie," I reveal reverently.

Her eyes flash open. Raising her head, she stares at me, first in shock, then her gaze is full of admiration. "I fell in love with you too, Drew."

A new kind of hunger ignites inside me, one only she can satisfy.

I take her hand, and together we lie down on the bed, facing one another. Our breathing is slightly more labored than before as we lie horizontally, our bare skin brushing lightly with every breath. I reach out tenderly, gliding my hand over every curve, moving around her and pulling her even closer to me. Her leg slides in between mine; our bodies entwine into one.

When a soft moan escapes her pink lips, I bring my mouth and cover hers to capture it. Our kiss is sensual, pure, gentle, and full of fire so bright I can feel the burn to the deepest parts of me.

When we touch and kiss every inch of exposed skin, I roll us until I'm hovering over her. Dipping my head, I kiss her hard and deep, our tongues dancing to a new, more urgent rhythm. I hook my hand behind her knee and push into her, groaning at the rush of satisfaction filling me. "Drew." She gasps when I reach her very center then begins moving beneath me.

The passion I feel for her takes over, and we begin moving together, whispering each other's names with each thrust. Watching her flushed face, I'm struck by the love I feel for her. Not only the love but the connection. A connection I've never felt before and one I haven't hoped for in more than a decade.

I move faster and harder with the new revelation of feelings, enjoying every sound coming from her, and I bring her to the edge. Silently, I promise never to stop letting her feel my love and devotion for her. We consume one another until no one else exists.

"I love you." She gasps, and I push into her deeper.

Her words put me on the verge of my release when I feel Rosie tremble beneath me, moaning my name until the only sound coming from her mouth is a satisfied sigh. With a few more thrusts, I fall over the edge with her.

I allow myself to fall to her side, pulling her with me. "I love you too, Rosie. I'll never stop holding you close."

"And I'll never stop letting you," she whispers back.

Closing my eyes, I breathe her in, tightening my arms around her. She makes content sounds, and before long I can tell she has fallen asleep. So this is what it feels like to really love someone and know them. It's effortless to love her. This happened naturally between us. I've never been so happy.

My lips tip up in both corners, and I fall into a deep, contented sleep.

Epilogue

Rosie

Before I open my eyes, I listen to his heart beating beneath my ear as I lie across his warm chest.

I'm waking up to our morning after. Our first real morning after. And I need a minute. Just one. To savor the feeling of having him here with me without doubts. Without unspoken words. Without any rules dictating how and what we should or can feel for one another.

Forty-five seconds to listen to him breathe. To enjoy the sound of his calm.

Thirty seconds to embrace the start of something new. Something wonderful. Something I can trust.

Fifteen seconds to remember I'm here because he loves me. The real me. The awkward, plain, and often scattered me.

Five seconds to remember I love him. The charming, occasionally cocky and laid-back Drew.

I take in my entire minute until there are no seconds left. But, it's okay because I'm the same girl who he fell asleep with last night and the same girl he woke up with this morning.

We've laid it all out. All the fear is gone. It's just the two of us. I close my eyes and drift back to sleep. Feeling safe.

I'm pretty sure Rosie was awake and just fell back to sleep. I can feel it in the way her breathing has changed. I don't open my eyes, though. I didn't let her know I was awake because I want to enjoy this moment of having her all to myself. In this quiet. Lying next to me. No panic. No fear.

I just need one minute. Only one.

I want this minute to appreciate this thing between us isn't about whether or not we can fall in love anymore because we've already fallen.

Forty-five seconds to recognize we've fallen slowly and freely.

Thirty seconds to remember I never want to experience another second without her.

Fifteen seconds to smile because I'm confident I won't ever need this kind of minute again.

Five seconds to repeat in my head, she loves me…she loves me…she loves me…she loves me…she loves me.

Reaching for her, I roll over and pull her to me. Closing my eyes, finding comfort in having her in my arms, and settling into a deep sleep.

When I open my eyes, Rosie is no longer lying beside me.

Drew: *Where are you?*
Rosie: *I'll be back soon. Go back to sleep.*
Drew: *Nice try. Why'd you leave me?*

Rosie: *I didn't leave you. I went to get us coffee and breakfast. In fact, look up.*

When I do as she says, Rosie is standing in the doorway to her bedroom, giving me the most beautiful grin.

Drew: *Hi.*
Rosie: *Why are you still texting me when I'm standing in front of you?*
Drew: *It's fun.*

She doesn't text me back. She doesn't say anything. Rosie only watches me, a content look on her face.

Drew: *What are you thinking about?*

The corner of her mouth quirks up and she shakes her head.

Drew: *Seriously, what are you thinking about?*
Rosie: *The morning after. You. Us. Our relationship.*
Drew: *What about the morning after? Me. Us. Our relationship.*
Rosie: *The morning after feels good. You're incredibly warm. I like us. And our relationship feels both new and old. Old, good. Not old, bad.*

I release a loud laugh.

Drew: *Okay. I get it. I never realized I liked morning afters until today. I think our relationship feels comfortable, which is why I'd like to think you think it feels old.*
Rosie: *How did we get here?*
Drew: *Fate?*

Rosie looks over at me for a brief second and smiles.

Rosie: *Fate? Really? What have you done with the commitment-phobe Drew Nallen I know and love.*
Drew: *You've cured me.*
Rosie: *That's sweet. You're sweet.*
Drew: *Describe our relationship in five words starting from the first moment we met until last night.*
Rosie: *5 words!!! Are you kidding me? This is going to be hard.*

I hear her sigh deeply from across the room.

Drew: *Hurry!*
Rosie: *Fine, here I go. Embarrassing. Friendly. Passionate. Longing. Whole.*

I'm stunned. She said it would be hard, but the words she chose are perfect. They let me know how she was feeling and I can pinpoint what time frame each represents, beginning to end.

Rosie: *Your turn, mister.*
Drew: *I'm not sure I can beat those, but I'll give it a go. Taken. Interested. Desire. Fearful. Brave.*

Almost immediately, Rosie jumps on top of me. As she looks down into my eyes, I see joy. Her eyes shimmer a little with tears.

"Drew, thank you for finally trusting me," she whispers, pressing her lips to mine.

When she pulls back, I smile up at her. "Rosie, I think I'm the one who should be thanking you for showing me I can love. And that love can be honest."

My hands cup her under her perky breasts, traveling over her rib cage, to her hips. She leans forward, touching her mouth to mine in a deep kiss. I pull her closer, and together we fall.

The End

ABOUT The Author

S hirl Rickman is a writer, a dreamer, and an optimist. A small town Texas girl currently residing in the San Francisco Bay Area with her beautifully blended family and their three crazy dogs. When she's not dreaming up new love stories, Shirl can be found reading and drinking way too much coffee. She loves kindness, laughing and meeting her readers.

Facebook:

https://www.facebook.com/shirlrickmanauthor/?pnref=story

Rickman's Rebels

https://www.facebook.com/groups/1010382209000750/

Twitter:

https://twitter.com/shirl_rickman

Instagram:

https://www.instagram.com/shirlrickmanauthor/